VANISHING

Also by the Author

Weather Woman
The Stylist
His Mother's Son

FIVE STORIES

Cai Emmons

VANISHING

Leapfrog Press
Fredonia, New York

Published in 2020 in the United States by
Leapfrog Press LLC
PO Box 505
Fredonia, NY 14063
www.leapfrogpress.com

Printed in the United States of America

Distributed in the United States by
Consortium Book Sales and Distribution
St. Paul, Minnesota 55114
www.cbsd.com

First Edition

Library of Congress Cataloging-in-Publication Data

Names: Emmons, Cai, author.
Title: Vanishing / Cai Emmons.
Description: First edition. | Fredonia, New York : Leapfrog Press, 2020. |
    Summary: "A new mother is bewildered when her house appears to belong to
    a stranger; a young artist must look past stereotypes to what really
    matters; a filmmaker visiting a childhood friend with dementia realizes
    how quickly shared history vanishes; an isolated young woman forms a
    manipulative friendship with a mother whose daughter has died; a
    middle-aged office manager discovers she isn't central in the lives of
    her adoring young male employees. These women's lives highlight the
    difficulty of honing a strong identity in a culture that consistently
    devalues women"-- Provided by publisher.
Identifiers: LCCN 2019047606 | ISBN 9781948585088 (paperback) | ISBN
    9781948585095 (ebook)
Classification: LCC PS3605.M57 A6 2020 | DDC 813/.6--dc23
LC record available at https://lccn.loc.gov/2019047606

And most women know this, that we are supposed to disappear, but it's something that needs to be said loudly, over and over again, so that we can resist surrendering to what is expected of us.

—Roxane Gay, *Hunger*

Contents

The Deed

When I stepped into the foyer after work I expected to hear the silence of Martin's absence, or rather I expected to hear the amplified sounds of my own actions ricocheting about the empty house, but instead I heard the grandfather clock ticking unevenly. I stood still for a moment, hushing the twins who, sensing something, grew tranquil and heavy at my hips. Yes, the ticking of the clock was distinctly uneven. Some of its beats were loud and others were light, giving it a slightly syncopated sound.

I suppose it was about a minute that I stood there, puzzling over the clock. It was the strangest feeling, akin to what it's like to arrive at your desk and know, from a brief or a pen that is out of alignment that someone has been there, tampering with things in your absence. The most bewildering aspect was that the clock showed the correct time, 6:53.

I had to get on with things, of course—the girls were hungry and beginning to fuss—so I forgot about the clock, or perhaps, more precisely, I shoved the clock problem aside. It was an old clock dating back to the early 1800's and it was natural that it should need some attention after all the years that Martin and

I had ignored it. I jotted it on the list, the list I was keeping for Martin.

I'm not one of those fanatical people who expect lists to solve all their problems; I simply think they're useful for keeping life orderly, for fending off encroaching chaos. Like countries having borders. Anyway, the first thing on my list was: *Overly bold birds?* In the morning when I was leaving the house four or five blue jays had flown in a pack onto the porch steps. They had lingered there, pecking at the floorboards and cackling like voyeuristic old men, as if they didn't intend to leave. When I shooed them away with my foot, they allowed me to make contact with their bodies and I found their solidity and boldness frightening. They weren't aggressive like the birds in the Hitchcock film, but they seemed stronger than I was.

The second thing on my list was: *Grandfather clock, uneven ticking.* Once I write something down I can usually stop thinking about it.

I lowered Beatrice into her high chair and gave her a piece of zwieback, then went to get Gina who I'd left on the floor with some measuring spoons. Gina's pudgy hand, fingers splayed like a starfish, reached out for me. I saw the faint red smudge on her wrist—a stork's bite, the doctor called it. It wasn't Gina after all, it was Beatrice, *she* was the one with the mark. I'd never made that mistake before, not since a few days after they were born.

Rattled, I shoveled rice cereal into their mouths, berating myself, not daring to yearn so soon for Martin's return. I don't like it when Martin is away, but I've always prided myself on being able to manage. The secret is keeping busy, adhering to a strict routine. Before he leaves I make sure my suits are cleaned and pressed, my nails are freshly manicured, my hair is trimmed. As an attorney, it is part of my profession to remain alert to things that may go wrong, but it is also my policy not

The Deed

to dwell on those things in Martin's absence. It is not helpful to articulate what I know to be true—that every moment our lives are only a hair's breadth from spinning out of control.

I gave the twins their baths and read them a story, and thankfully they went to sleep without much fussing. I listened for Beatrice who is usually the one to squawk after the lights go out, but even she went down easily. That made me feel good. I distinctly remember descending the staircase feeling a sheen of accomplishment, thinking I did have control of things and would get through Martin's absence just fine after all.

Downstairs in the kitchen I decided I was entitled to a drink. I know it's usually considered a sign of unhappiness to drink alone, but at that moment I was not unhappy. I wanted a drink because I felt satisfied and thought I should celebrate the feeling. I opened a bottle of Chardonnay. I'm not knowledgeable about wines—that's Martin's department—but I couldn't help noticing that this bottle, a California wine, was probably good, as it cost almost twenty dollars. I hoped Martin wasn't saving it for some special occasion.

As soon as the glass was poured and the corked bottle was restored to the fridge, I heard the TV pop on. For a minute I froze. It flew through my mind that it might be the neighbors' TV I was hearing but, though our neighbors on one side can sometimes be loud, I'd never heard their TV sounding as if it was right in our house. I considered that a burglar could be responsible for the sound, but I didn't hear any rifling about and of course why would a burglar (unless he was completely psychotic) enter a house and turn on the TV? It didn't make sense. A mechanical problem then? A short circuit? The TV had tripped on like a car alarm responding to a bolt of thunder? Perhaps the popping of the wine cork had done it.

So, after a period of time—undoubtedly less than a minute—when my mind was sorting these possibilities, I headed for the living room, still holding onto this (in retrospect) some-what far-fetched thought about the TV having been tripped on by the audible popping of the wine cork.

When I got to the hallway, I noticed the living room light was on. It had not been on when we arrived home—that I knew—and I was certain I hadn't turned it on since. I am very thrifty and try hard not to waste electricity. So the fear I had so successfully laid aside a moment earlier rose again, and (I am ashamed to say) my first impulse was to cry out for Martin. But I restrained myself and instead hugged the wall of the foy-er. That was when I first heard the sound of a person moving. How instinctively programmed we are to recognize the sounds of human movement. Someone was rising from the couch and walking to the door. Someone was in the house with me.

I thought of screaming, but for what? It would only scare the girls. And, terrified as I was, I felt foolish raising my voice, so I pressed my face against the wall as if it would hide me. Then, into the stretch of floor included in my vision stepped a pair of sneakered feet.

"Can I help you?" asked a male voice.

I'm sure I looked ridiculous, clutching the wall and gaping at this man as I did. But what was I to think when a perfect stranger addressed me that way in my own house?

As men go, he was rather harmless-looking. He was possibly thirty years old (a little younger than I). Neither tall nor short, he had the densely muscled body of a weight lifter. He wore khaki trousers, old-fashioned white sneakers, and a maroon V-necked sweater that looked as if it might be cashmere. Neat but casual clothes, the clothes of a relaxing professional, not a criminal. He stood watching me patiently, no observable alarm marring the symmetry of his features. Embarrassed, I stood up straight. In the living room I heard the sudden rise in the TV's volume as the ads took over from the program.

The Deed

"Can I help you?" he said.

"Who are you?" I demanded.

"Cute." He took my upper arm in a forceful grip and led me to the door. "Don't worry, I won't press charges."

"Press charges?" I shook off his hand and faced him. He seemed taller than he had at first and his body blocked off my view of the rest of the house.

"I'm curious, though, how did you get in?" he asked.

A terrible helplessness came over me, reducing my voice to a whimper.

"My purse is upstairs, take what you want. But please get out." I panted. A pulse in my neck jittered. His gaze scanned my body before he began chuckling. Then he stepped back from me and held out his arm, extending it to the stairway.

"All right, we'll find that purse of yours."

I didn't move. "My husband will be home soon you know."

He nodded. "The purse?"

I knew it was always the best policy to give these people whatever they wanted, but I hesitated, thinking of the girls asleep upstairs. I did not want to leave him downstairs alone, nor did I want to allow him into the bedroom with me. He was not unsavory and he had curiously good manners, but there was a businessman's callousness about him, and it did not take much imagination to picture him hurling me onto the bed and having his way with me.

I went because I saw no choice. I plodded up the stairs sideways, keeping my eye on him. He returned my look calmly. I prayed that the twins would not awaken.

He stood courteously outside the bedroom while I searched for my purse. What caught my attention instead was a man's suit lying over the easy chair on Martin's side of the room. It was not Martin's suit. Martin never wore gray suits so I knew it wasn't his. Could it really belong to this man?

13

So distracted was I by the suit that I couldn't find my purse, and then I remembered that I'd left it downstairs. I told him this and he smiled an irritating power smile as if he didn't care where it was since he knew he'd get it eventually. We paraded back down to the kitchen. There was my purse on the telephone table. I found the wallet and handed it to him.

"Now you can go," I said.

His smile, or I should say sneer, wouldn't go away now. He opened my wallet and looked through it, scrutinizing each credit card approvingly before he looked for the cash. When he got to the compartment for bills he spread it open and held it up to my view. Nothing.

"How generous of you," he said.

"I meant to stop at the cash machine. We can go there now if you want."

"I see we've been sampling the goods," he said, nodding to my untouched glass of wine on the counter. He slipped the wallet back into my handbag, laid the handbag on the table, and handed me the glass of wine.

"Finish the wine and go. I have some people coming. This episode will amuse them."

I drank the wine because I did not know what else to do. I was thinking about the word *episode*.

"We all have our stories, don't we," he said. "Tell me, you look well enough off, what motivates a woman like you to do something like this?"

I told him I wasn't going to dignify his question with an answer, and then the telephone rang. What a relief; it was Martin, I knew. He often called at just this hour. But, when I reached for the phone the man took it from my hand, not aggressively, but firmly.

"Vern Hallohan speaking." He answered with casual indifference.

The Deed

I could hear the buzz of the voice on the other end, and I knew it was not Martin—it was someone who fully expected this Vern Hallohan to answer.

"Yes, whenever you can is fine, I'll be here. Good, looking forward to it. . . . No, Mergers and Acquisitions. Right, bye."

"That was for you?" I said when he had hung up.

"You thought it was who? Your husband?" He chuckled softly.

I knew I had to take charge. The wine had braced me. "If you don't leave the house by the count of five, I'm calling the police."

"Oh, please."

I abhorred his tone of voice. It was the disdainful tone that mothers use with intractable children, that some of my male colleagues have used with me from time to time. "I mean it," I said. "One . . . two . . ."

"What will you say to the police?"

"That you're here, that you broke in, that you won't leave."

He shook his head as if I were truly pathetic. "What a sorry fellow—he won't leave his own house."

At that moment I came as close as I've ever come to hitting someone, but of course I didn't. "I'm going to reiterate the obvious—this isn't your house," I said.

"Oh?"

"It's *my* house."

"I'm happy to go through this charade with you if it will make you happy, but let's see who the police are likely to believe. Prima facie. *Who* found *who* sneaking around? Do you even have a key for this house?"

"Of course I have a key." I pawed around in my bag but my keys were snuggled somewhere out of reach. I heard a click as he laid something on the counter.

"That could be any key," I said.

"Yes, but it isn't, is it?" He went to the front door and slid his key smoothly into the lock.

I felt myself sinking beneath the quicksand of our misunderstandings. "My babies are upstairs."

"Your babies are upstairs?"

"Why would I break in here with children?"

He trailed me up there and, to my great relief, Beatrice and Gina were still there, sleeping soundly. I put my ear down into each of their cribs to confirm that they were still breathing.

"See?" I said.

"See what? This proves nothing. You brought your babies here, that's all. I give you credit for ingenuity. Not that that will hold any water with the police."

"With cribs," I pointed out, feeling more and more confused. I was still wondering what I could have done with my keys.

"These cribs have always been here. For my girlfriend's children. I take it somehow you knew that?"

He picked up a blanket that had fallen off the edge of Gina's crib. He folded it and put it in the bottom drawer of the dresser right alongside the rest of the blankets! It could, of course, have been a lucky accident, but it disturbed me because it coincided with something else I'd noticed. He did not move about the house as if he were a stranger to it; he negotiated the sharp angles and creaky floorboards as if he knew them, as if he'd been moving around here for years.

It sounds absurd, but I could see he really believed this house was his. I could see it in the unyielding opacity of his eyes, in his immutable body, and in his sneering but decorous manner. He was being tolerant of me because he believed himself. It was now up to me to demonstrate the fallacy of his case.

He must have spotted a change in me because quite suddenly he suggested we go downstairs to the living room to talk. I followed him down. He swung through the kitchen and took the wine bottle and two glasses. He knew exactly which cupboard held the glassware.

The Deed

In the living room he set the bottle and glasses on the coffee table next to a bowl of popcorn; then he used the remote control to turn off the TV which was playing a baseball game.

"If it's your house, where were you this morning?" I said.

"Here."

"And last night?"

"Here."

Clearly a pointless line of questioning, but I was rattled and my logic had gone haywire. I watched him pick stray kernels of popcorn from the cracks between the couch cushions, his fingers scratching around like a pecking chicken. A precise, almost finicky person, I could tell. This action both fascinated and irritated me, but most of all it called up a strange flicker of recognition.

"Are you an attorney?" I asked suddenly.

He nodded hesitantly.

"Where do you work?"

He paused for a moment, considering the wisdom of answering. "Ostrow, Reichert and Burton."

I nodded. `ORB,' we called them at work. "I've seen you then." I did not mention that his firm was the opposing representation on my 10-B Haines Realty case.

"Oh?" He was pouring the wine now. He handed me a glassful.

"I work for Bartlett, Boggins, Pipkin, and Spitzer."

He squinted at me. "For?"

"Bartlett, Boggins, Pipkin and Spitzer."

"I mean which attorney do you work for?"

"I *am* an attorney."

"I see." He sipped his wine. I didn't have to be Einstein to see that he neither recognized nor believed me, but my own memory of him was becoming more and more distinct. I could picture him sitting at the end of our conference table, digging into the cherry molding with his pencil. The action had annoyed me then—I suppose he was not relenting on some point; I don't recall exactly—and when I saw him pick up those popcorn kernels, I had no doubt this was the same man.

"An attorney," he repeated and the sneer returned to his face. I felt I was at work, in a meeting at the conference table with fifteen men who made me half invisible and half a laughing stock, who would never make me partner, and who habitually saved their best jokes until after I left the room.

I was drinking the wine without meaning to. I knew it was whittling away the legal acumen I needed, but at the moment it was the only way I had to calm myself. It drove me crazy that we were there chatting like perfectly normal logical people. Or rather I was treating him like a logical person, though he was hardly returning the favor.

"Okay," I said, "do you have the deed?"

"The deed. The lady wants the deed."

"If you can show me a deed, I'll leave." I knew I had him then. What was he going to do, draw up a deed right then and there?

He got up and left the room. I heard him climbing the stairs. What if he did something to the twins? I started after him. Then I heard his footsteps tramping into Martin's study, followed by the metallic shiver of a file cabinet drawer lurching open. Was he honestly looking for his supposed deed in Martin's file cabinet?

I returned to the living room. Next door I could see the silhouetted bodies of our elderly neighbors, the Maxwells, moving around their living room. When they turned out their lights I felt unbearably alone. A sudden impulse carried me outside, across the lawn, and onto the Maxwells' porch. Their outdoor light went off just as I arrived at the front door. I knocked anyway. I could hear muffled voices, but it was at least a full minute before the door opened.

The Deed

Mr. Maxwell peered through a crack, then he recognized me and opened the door wide. He wore a red plaid bathrobe and his expression was puzzled. We don't see much of the Maxwells, so he was understandably surprised. Mrs. Maxwell was saying something inaudible in the background. He glanced at her.

"It's the lady from next door." Then he turned back to me. "Yes, dear, how can I help?" His voice was tired and reedy.

"Well, it's a little hard to explain—" He looked so stooped and sallow I began to question the point of my solicitation.

"Yes?"

Knowing I had to say something, I tried to order the events. "When I came home today there was someone in my house."

"Oh dear. Shall we call the police? What did he take? You aren't hurt are you?"

"Oh no, it's not—" I paused. How could I say it? "He's not exactly a criminal. I mean he might be, but he's very well-dressed and polite and all. And he's an attorney—"

I lost my train of thought. Vern was alone in our house, alone with the girls. How irresponsible of me to leave.

"I'm sorry, I have to get back. I'm so sorry."

Mr. Maxwell frowned. "Have you called the police?"

"No."

"Would you like me to?"

"Well—" I thought of Vern looking for his deed. What if he had one? Not that I thought he did but . . . I sighed. "It's so complicated. I'm really so sorry to have bothered you."

I turned and hurried down the steps, pausing for a reassuring wave when I got to the pavement. Then I dashed home.

Vern stood in the living room near the window that looks out to the Maxwells. He eyed me as I tried to recover my breath. From the superior little smile he wore I realized he'd probably been watching me over there and perhaps knew what had transpired. As for his deed, I didn't see it, but before he sat back down on the couch he reached into his pocket and withdrew a sheet of folded parchment paper which he handed to me. It was indeed a deed, bearing the address of the premises and his name, Vernon Leroy Hallohan. It bore a date from two years earlier.

Out of the corner of my eye, I could see him leaning back on the couch, sipping his wine and watching me gloatingly. After that, my mind wouldn't settle properly. It was not possible that we both owned these premises. Had Martin sold the house without my knowing?

Vern radiated a terrible, forceful calm. I saw he was not an imposter. His ownership was palpable. Certainty leached from me; everything I had known for sure only hours before, now crumbled around me.

I did not rip up his deed; I handed it back to him. I went upstairs and bundled the twins into quilts. They moaned a little and stared at me. How solemn their pursed matching mouths looked! How large their eyes! It was almost as if they did not trust me to do things correctly. I put on a warm coat and, purse in hand and one twin under each arm, I went outside without bothering to look for Vern again.

The other houses on the block were dark and the streetlight outside our house must have had a short circuit because it was flickering off and on like a lighthouse beacon. I went to the car which was parked on the street in front of the house. As soon as I got there, I remembered in a panic that my keys were missing, but now when I checked my purse they were there in the usual place. I wanted to cry out from relief and confusion. Had he put them back there? Had I simply overlooked them?

With some difficulty, I lowered the back seats so the girls could lie flat. Then I got into the driver's seat, but I didn't start the ignition, I just sat there, trembling, thinking about Martin and wondering if he was still alive. What I felt was not fear—I had already passed through that—but an overpowering sense of dislocation.

Every once in a while I looked back at the twins. Once, I caught Beatrice's eyes, round and reflective and breakable as Christmas tree ornaments, and I thought: *These precious girls are all I have left.* I brought Beatrice into the front seat with me, thinking if I left her awake by herself in the back she would die from loneliness.

After a while, I saw the light in the living room go off. I put Beatrice in the back again, started the car, and drove a little way down the street until the house was barely visible. Lying across the two front seats, coccyx against the gearshift, back bridging the chasm between the bucket seats, I tried to sleep. The light from the streetlights would not stay still, but moved in lurid waves that penetrated my lids. I suppose I must have dozed a little because I recall a nightmarish dream.

I was in the house talking to Vern Hallohan and suddenly various men from my firm started appearing. They sauntered into the room with drinks and seated themselves, ignoring me. After a while, I began to realize they could not even see me. Vern began laughing. He seized one of the pillows from the couch and rubbed it across his face, removing a layer of dark makeup. Underneath the makeup, the man was Martin.

I awoke with a start, filled with a thought I'd never had before. Did Martin want, deep down, to leave me? In the dark I fumbled for my cell phone, which I knew was in my purse. Sometimes it is a reassuring device, but that night it wasn't. I felt sure it would connect me to bad news. It was late, I knew, but with Martin that wouldn't matter. Then, just as I was about to call, I thought of the way I might sound, my voice thin, squeaky perhaps, the voice of a woman without command, incapable of conducting her business alone. I couldn't help thinking of a thing that had happened the morning he left. It was a small thing but nonetheless notable. He was sitting at the kitchen table, drinking his coffee, and I was feeding the girls their cereal. I alternate spoonfuls—one to Gina, one to Beatrice, one to Gina, one to Beatrice, and so on. In between my spoonfuls they try to feed themselves with their hands, and their faces, admittedly, become quite comically messy. Usually Martin doesn't notice. But that morning something caused him to glance over at us. His face was hard with disdain. Martin is a kind, mild man; he never looks disdainful. "Can't you clean them up a bit?" he said. His voice sounded momentarily irate, savage even, but then he smiled and turned back to his coffee as if he was only making a joke. For an instant I could not move, but right away, of course, I came back to life. He is an accountant and very precise, and I am also very precise, but less so than Martin. Remembering this moment again in the car, I found it almost a relief to discover my cell phone battery was dead. Later, I dozed briefly again, but my arm fell asleep and the numbness awakened me. I sat up to readjust my position. My gaze was drawn to the house. I felt as if the girls and I were all part of a satellite drifting in a lazy orbit around that place. I didn't want to look, I didn't mean to look, but there I was, looking. Even from this distance I could tell the whole house was ablaze with light and I remembered how he'd said he was having people over. I glanced at my watch. Two-thirty, Tuesday morning. I considered going to investigate, but to what end? To gaze at a house I could no longer call my own?

I rolled down the window and heard music playing. It thrummed with an insistent bass line. I did not go to sleep after that. I sat up with my head bent over the steering wheel, waiting for the girls to stir. They awakened with the sun, wet and hungry and agitated by the strange surroundings. I'd left the house so hastily that I had no food or diapers, so I had to distract them by singing crazily. Exhaustion snaked behind my eyes. Around seven-thirty people began emerging from their houses to go to work and I knew I had to move.

The girls had made me giddy and I wasn't sure I should be driving, but of course in moments like that you pull yourself together. As I started the car, I avoided looking down the street toward the house, but I caught a brief glimpse of myself in the rearview mirror—limp sweaty hair, eyes made grotesque from hours of foreboding—and I panicked. There was no place to look.

I drove to the babysitter's at fifteen miles per hour, keeping my eyes on the rectangle of pavement immediately in front of my bumper. The girls were crying in high-pitched yelps that told me how disconcerted they were.

I stood on the babysitter's porch gripping the twins, leaning desperately on the buzzer and trying to suppress the thought that perhaps she no longer lived here and someone else, a complete stranger, would answer the door. I smelled urine, I wasn't sure whose.

"Heavens!" she said when she opened the door. "What happened?" She took the twins and looked for the diaper bag, but saw that I didn't have it.

"I have to run," I said. "I'll explain everything later."

I went out to the car and drove a few blocks to a commercial district where I parked in the back of a dry cleaner's and sat for a long time. The door to the dry cleaning establishment was wide open, and I heard the giant machines slapping the clothes around. The fumes permeated the car even though the windows were closed. Finally, I convinced myself to get out. I walked gingerly into the cleaner's. A man with a thick Indian accent stood behind the desk. He regarded me warily and hesitated when I asked to use the phone. "Please," I begged. "Something bad—" I flung an arm out toward the street, a gesture he couldn't possibly have interpreted in any meaningful way, but he pointed toward his landline, no doubt pitying me, and allowed me to come behind the desk and watched me as I called my office and told them I was ill and would not be in that day.

Then I returned to our neighborhood to examine the situation in the light of day. I drove by the house, amazed to see it still standing. I rounded the block twice, three times, before I finally stopped. Perhaps I should have enlisted someone's help before going inside, but I knew from the way I looked that my credibility would be in question. Instead I took the tire iron from the trunk, just in case.

Of course I was as careful as could be. I didn't go inside until I had verified from the outside that the place appeared empty. My key worked as usual and I stood breathlessly in the foyer, waiting for the house to speak. The grandfather clock ticked out its usual metronomic beat. Everything looked so neat. I began in the living room. The coffee table was clean and unblemished. I lifted the couch cushions to search for popcorn kernels, but found none. The kitchen was also spotless. No wine glasses in the drainer or the dishwasher and, when I checked the cupboard, I found all twelve of them settled complacently in their usual corner.

Then upstairs. I can picture how strange I must have looked mounting the stairs with a tire iron held high in striking position. The suit was gone from the chair in the bedroom. The bed was made. There was nothing amiss in the bathroom or in the girls' room. The blanket Vern Hallohan had folded was lying in the drawer where he'd put it. Of course I opened every closet, looked under every bed, even peered behind the extra blankets in the linen closet. I made sure each door and window was locked. Then I took a shower, put on some clean clothes, and called a locksmith.

While I waited for the locksmith I went to find the deed,

The Deed

our deed. I wasn't sure where Martin kept it, but his file cabinet seemed a likely possibility. Under H I found a folder for "HOUSE." I rifled through it. Sure enough, there was the deed. It had both of our names on it and the date—September 27, 2014—the day we'd bought the house. I knew it!

I had Mr. Vern Hallohan now. If he came back for a visit tonight, he would be locked out and I would be armed with my tire iron and my deed. His deed would count for nothing then.

I did not leave the house all day. The babysitter obliged me by bringing the girls home, realizing from my appearance that morning that something dreadful was at stake.

Vern Hallohan did not appear that evening, that night, or the next morning. By the third day I felt ready to risk a return to work. When I arrived at my desk I sat for some time, staring at the neat undisturbed piles I'd left, the stiletto points of the pencils my secretary, Janet, had sharpened just so. I noticed a gray slug-shaped stain on my blotter and I scraped at it with my fingernail. I like a pristine blotter and the stain irritated me, but I needed to forget about it and catch up with my work. I pulled the paper pile toward me and began reading. The case at the top of the pile was a stock fraud case, not an uncommon case for our firm to handle. But this case I did not recall at all. In two days I had forgotten every detail of this dossier of briefs and documents. Usually my memory is irreproachable—sometimes I think my entire intelligence has to do with the precision of my memory—but that day, when I tried to remember the particulars of this case I could not. I labored for the better part of an hour with a series of self quizzes. How long have you had this case? What is the trial date? Who were you working with? Who is the opposing representation? I could not answer any of these questions from memory. What are the names of your children? I asked myself. What is your husband's name? The answers to these last questions were still, thank god, accessible.

I knew, in order to calm myself, I had to turn my attention to a case with which I was conversant. I looked for the Haines Realty case. That case I had worked on obsessively for close to two months. I'd taken all the depositions, done most of the research and discovery. I knew it better than anyone at the firm, even better than Payne Whipple, the partner in charge. But the Haines dossier was not in my pile. I checked my file cabinet. It was not there. I checked every shelf and drawer in the office. It was not to be found.

With great reluctance I summoned Janet. She is a stocky, efficient woman with a no-nonsense manner and intelligent eyes that notice details. At times I have thought she would make a better attorney than I. She is deferential to me in all observable ways, but she understands my position at the office and sometimes regards me with such unabashed pity that I am loathe to ask her help too frequently.

I spoke to her in a low voice. "Janet, I've misplaced the dossier on the Haines Realty case."

"He didn't leave you a note? Mr. Whipple took it when you were away. He said there was deadline pressure."

"He said that?"

She nodded. She waited for my next request without affect.

"There wasn't," I said. "There was no deadline pressure. There are still two full months before the trial."

She shrugged. "Talk to Mr. Whipple."

She looked at me strangely and I realized I was leaning forward, ducking my head, speaking almost conspiratorially. I jerked back up.

"Of course," I said.

I dismissed her and put on my suit jacket. I fluffed the shoulder pads and dusted a few flakes of dandruff off the lapels. Was this how they fired you, taking your cases one by one until your desk was empty? I stood with my palms on my desk, as if I

planned to spring to action. But I didn't. I weighed the benefits
of speaking to Payne, versus those of letting the case go without comment. If I hadn't sensed Janet at her desk outside my
office taking measure of my courage, I wouldn't have gone.
Head high, arms in a military swing, I strode past her. On the
maroon plush carpet my shoes were soundless. By the time I
turned the corner onto Payne's corridor, my arms hung like
noodles and there was nothing vaguely military about me.

Payne was at his desk, pencil flying. I stayed outside but
extended my head into the office margin. After a moment he
looked up.

"Yes?" he said, almost as if I were a complete stranger.

"I'm back."

He stared at me for a long moment. Then he said, "Glad
to hear it." His voice was neutral, almost flat. He returned to
work. I hovered there a moment staring at his thick pin-striped
forearms. I took a few steps backward, then forward.

He looked up again, realizing I had not left. I felt perhaps
he was irritated.

"Do you know Vern Hallohan?" I said.

"Guy at ORB?"

"Yes."

"Think I've met him. Once or twice. Look, I'd love to chat,
but you know how it is."

I nodded. My understandings flew away from me like tenu-
ous threads in a stiff wind. I drifted as quietly as I could down
the corridor. The following week I tendered my resignation,
and I have not returned to work since, plagued by a feeling that
even after a decade of practicing law I am not, and maybe never
have been, suited to it.

I've never told Martin about this. When he asked me why I'd
changed the locks, I said I'd lost my key. For a while I considered saying more, but then I wondered why no one—neither

the babysitter nor the Maxwells—had said a word to me afterwards. No one asked me if I was all right or if things had settled down. The world is like that these days—terrible and confusing things happen, but no one blinks an eye or even tries to clarify what went wrong. So why bother Martin with it? He would only be dismayed and tell me what I already know—that I've been too timid about what's really mine.

About ten days after Martin returned, I stepped onto the porch early one morning to get the Sunday paper. It was frosty out, a day beautifully burnished by cold, and as soon as the air hit my face I felt bright-eyed. There wasn't any action on the street, and I stood there for a moment reveling in the rare peace. Then, I heard Martin calling me from inside, telling me I was letting in the cold, so I reached down for the paper. As I crouched something caught my eye. Laced into the corner created by the pillar and the porch railing was an exquisite silky spider web, swaying gently. It caught the light, tossing it about playfully so it winked and sparkled and tried to break free. It was a dazzling sight and I was amazed that it had escaped me until now. I wondered if my phone's camera could possibly capture this spectacle.

I snatched the paper and rose from my kneeling position. The spider web disappeared. I blinked and squinted, but it wasn't there. Slowly, I lowered myself again onto my haunches, and the web came back into view, as arresting as it had been a second before. I raised and lowered myself a few more times. Each time the web came into view at precisely the same place, revealing itself to me not piece by piece, but as one fully formed creation. There, not there, there, not there, there, not there.

FAT

She thought she was grownup at twenty, but on that first day of Life Drawing she stood in the doorway and saw immediately how deluded she'd been. The other students were all older, in their thirties, or even forties. They wore black as if they'd invented it. Tasha wished she had a hat to cover her ridiculous platinum hair, a last-minute choice she'd made before leaving LA. The teacher nodded her in and pointed her to one of the empty easels. His name was Rupert Pimble, and he was supposedly famous, though she'd never heard of him. He wore an unbuttoned gray cardigan and little black shoes that looked like ballet slippers. His hair ruffled out from under his black skull cap like a mangy gray bedskirt.

She entered with her head down. Only when she got to the designated easel did she look up to see the model arranging herself on a wooden platform at the center of the room. She had never seen anyone so fat. Fat slumped from this woman's bones like loose dough. A laugh tittered up from Tasha's belly, but she strangled it with a cough. She'd known the models would be naked, but she didn't expect *this*. This model was sumo wrestler fat. Circus sideshow fat. Crazy or diseased person fat. The kind of fat with its own vocal chords yelling: *Problems!*

Tasha averted her gaze and sloughed her bag and took off her jacket and tried to look busy, waiting for instructions. It was five minutes or so before she realized there would be no instructions. Everyone had already begun to draw, their charcoal a quiet scritching against the room's silence. Rupert shuffled from easel to easel, scrutinizing the work.

"Problems?" he said quietly when he came to her.

"I'm good." She raised her stick of charcoal and made a bold line on the paper to let him know he could move on. But he lingered.

"Don't look at the page," he said. "This is about the eye, not the hand."

She nodded. She'd taken plenty of art classes before.

"An exercise in *seeing*."

She nodded more emphatically, her hand frozen. She could say she wasn't a beginner, but something told her he wouldn't care.

"Get to it. Don't think." She nodded again and he shuffled off.

The model sat on the platform with one leg extended, the other knee bent so the sole of her foot touched the blob of her leg. She stared vacantly into a middle distance, eyes mere pellets in the quicksand of her face, the blonde hair that dusted her shoulders thin as shredded wheat. The rills and hillocks of her seemed vast as the Saharan desert.

The middle-aged woman at the easel next to Tasha was a dervish, as if this drawing was a race. It aroused a competitiveness Tasha wasn't used to feeling. In her high school art classes she'd always been the best—no one even came close—but when she was putting together her portfolio before coming east she worried she might only be a good technician, not a real artist. At

Fat

home teachers always gave her license to do things her own way. Here there was so much to get wrong.

She tried to focus, but Art-Tasha was absent, the girl who had always slid so easily into the work. She crossed her eyes to identify an overall shape on which to hang details. Circle? Triangle? She saw various objects. Tiers of belly fat like folded blankets. Breasts like full laundry bags. The hands were starfish, the head a fringed beach ball.

Everyone else was filling page after page. The minutes were darting by, and Rupert had already circled back to her again. Except for a few truncated lines, her page was still empty. Disdain bled through his silence. The room itself was a problem, high-ceilinged and mostly empty, naked really, a no-place place. Sun streamed through a bank of tall dusty windows facing 14th Street where traffic sounds rose in a constant babble of white noise.

"Okay, Jane," Rupert said. "New position, please."

Jane. The name seemed wrong, too plain for a woman whose very size made her complicated. The flipping tablets sent up a choral swish. Jane lugged herself to standing and stepped off the platform and lumbered to a corner of the room where a red bathrobe was draped over an electric wheelchair. Tasha was the only one watching. The other students chatted and sipped from water bottles and consulted their phones. Tasha imagined the people she knew in LA seeing this model. Brian, Francine, her mother. And Julian—god, he would die.

Jane located a liter of Diet Coke and a bag of Jolly Ranchers on the floor. She took a swig of the Coke and unwrapped a Jolly Rancher and popped it into her mouth then returned to the platform and lowered herself to sitting again. She swayed as tethered elephants do. Her eyes shifted slightly, their focus sharpening, roving, then landing on Tasha. Tasha stiffened. She wanted to look away but couldn't—their gazes were glued. What was Jane seeing? Her eyes jerked away, but already it was too late. Jane had seen what she'd seen.

She rose to all fours and angled herself so her crinkly rump and thighs faced Tasha directly. Her private parts were concealed, but to Tasha Jane's entire body was one massive private part. Rupert brought towels and, quietly solicitous, helped Jane arrange them under her knees.

It was time to resume drawing. Again Tasha couldn't begin. She was thinking of Julian. When they were together back in LA he was trying to lose weight. He was an actor and thought being thinner would help him get parts. After they made love, drowsing in the sheets, he would pinch the skin of his belly, grimacing in self-disgust. When he stroked her bottom she could feel him measuring her too, for self-control and strength of character.

But Jane. It must take strength of character to crouch naked in front of a class. How many people, even beautiful skinny people, had the strength to do that?

Rupert was talking to the woman beside Tasha. "Exactly," he said. Tasha wanted to peek at the woman's work, but couldn't without being too intrusive.

Tasha was the first to leave when the class was over. She hurtled out of there without saying a word to anyone, and descended to the street feeling horribly young and too emotional. No one here cared if she lived or died. She'd never been in a place where people had reacted so little to her presence. She was used to stirring things up. Even her mother hadn't called. Not that Tasha wanted to speak to her mother, but shouldn't she have called?

Her drawing tablet was heavy. She dumped it into the first trash can she came to, the entire day's work—what little there was—gone, along with the unused pages. It was after 5:00, but everyone on the street was amped up as if the day was just beginning. She didn't want to go home—if you could call the Roses' place home. Once there she'd have to hibernate in that boy's smelly room.

The room on Rivington Street was small and dark, and it looked out on a brick wall. By LA standards it was terrible, but Tasha, knowing she was lucky to have landed a place in Manhattan, was trying to see things in a positive light. Everyone had told her she'd have to live far from the city—in Brooklyn, or Queens, or New Jersey—so she was grateful to the Roses who'd rented her this room after their son left for college. She tried to make herself invisible, coming and going quietly, using the kitchen only when they weren't there. Sometimes they invited her to join them at dinner, but she wasn't sure they meant it. They were short, retiring, university people, their faces long and pale, their backs hunched. They couldn't be more different from her embarrassing mother, and she felt self-conscious around them, acutely aware of being young and uneducated, potentially too loud, and still carrying the extra weight she always meant to be losing. No, thanks, she'd say. Then she'd go out and get matzoh ball soup around the corner.

At night, alone in the small room that still smelled vaguely of boy, she could hear the Roses rustling around, doing god knows what. It made her more desperate than ever to make something of herself as an artist. It was a horrible thought that she might end up with a life as colorless as theirs.

She was walking faster than usual, and it felt good. She was learning the pedestrian dance, the art of avoiding sidewalk collisions, side-stepping, leaping forward, looping around slow-moving clusters. Each step edged her closer to erasing thoughts of Jane and Rupert but, in exchange, loneliness rose up from the pavement and inflamed her entire body. She tried not to gawk. Did people come to this city to be anonymous, or to prove they were not?

She thought she might not go back to class, but she'd already paid for three months from the stash of money she saved while working at the Gap. And she'd come here for this. Monday, Wednesday, Friday, 2-5:00, a regular chunk of time that buttressed her otherwise wide-open life. She'd put in some applications for retail jobs in Soho, Nolita, the West Village, but every place kept telling her the same thing, check back next week.

Sometimes Rupert wasn't in class, but the students and a model were always there. No one skipped—this wasn't high school. A couple of times she overslept and arrived late and when she entered Rupert shook his head, *tut-tut.* Sometimes he stationed himself behind her easel, singling her out with quiet admonishments. *Draw what you see, not what you want to see. Not what you think you see.*

The models were never normal. After the fat woman there was a twenty-something guy with a bald head tinted yellow and tattoos over his whole body like skintight clothing. His dick wasn't tattooed, but it had a bolt-sized piercing that made you wince. Then there was a very old man whose thighs were smeared with pale fuzz. They had all mastered that same vacant stare, a look that eliminated the students with the pretense of not caring.

The other students were drawing machines. They, too, stared at the models with a kind of indifference. Tasha imagined them drawing away as the world ended and fire engulfed them. She tried to emulate their diligence but didn't think she was learning anything. She no longer threw her work away, mainly because it was a waste of money—the cost of materials was the students' responsibility and it added up—but she didn't review her work either. The filled tablets began to take up space under her bed at the Roses'. When she felt bleak, she thought of calling Julian, remembering how his eyes had always looked to her like aquariums, full of darting movement and trembling light, a medium for secrets. He didn't know she was here. Julian with hair like a black sheep and shredding blue eyes. Vain Julian who was *so ful-*

Fat

ly devoted to his art. Well, he wasn't the only fully devoted one.

She was on her way home through Washington Square Park. It was October and getting colder, and the wind was savage. She was thinking of her mother's love for extreme things. She still missed the times she and her mother would, out of the blue, drop everything they were supposed to do and summon Mr. Fun. Mr. Fun sessions usually meant a drive somewhere—the beach or the desert—and they often included ice cream.

Under the arch a woman in a wheelchair was staring at the sidewalk. A green wool blanket made a puffy plain of her lap, the wind made flotsam of her blonde hair. *Jane*, Tasha realized, the fat model. Something appeared to be wrong—the stillness, the downcast gaze.

Tasha circled the park and entered again. Jane was still there, in the same place, weirdly stationary in the blasting wind. Tasha followed Jane's eye-line to a phone on the sidewalk.

"Is that yours?"

Jane looked up. Her eyes, tiny and smart, were blackened by sunlight. "Fugue state. Yes, it's mine."

Tasha handed Jane the phone and Jane, all business, nodded her gratitude, not copping to any need. She stashed the phone in a large brown purse tucked on one side of her lap and started to roll off, the sturdy chair traveling seamlessly over the sidewalk cracks. After a short distance, she braked and swiveled. "Do I know you?"

Tasha, caught staring, shook her head. "I don't think so. No."

Jane's face registered nothing—no recognition, no relief, no gratitude, no interest in connection—and she took off.

Two days later, Jane was back in class again, naked of course, with the same red robe and liter of Diet Coke and bag of Jolly Ranchers. This time her face was heavily made up, cheeks blazing with rouge, blue eye shadow, hot pink lips. She assumed a position on her back, lifting various body parts and laying them down like luggage. Her eyes, the intense scalding tips of branding irons, caught sight of Tasha. "Fuck you," she said softly, but everyone heard.

Tasha was the first to arrive at the Chelsea café near where Julian was rehearsing a play.

She took a table and waited, eyeing other people's plates of sparkling Danishes and chocolate-covered croissants, feeling a wolfish hunger.

Julian had always called himself *punctilious*. Was he standing her up? She ordered a mocha with whipped cream. He walked in just as she was licking a fingerful. In thigh-length black coat, bright cobalt shirt, and neon-green scarf, he popped out from the blandness around him. His springy black curls had been trimmed. The nine months he'd been here had made him more shiny in that blue-eyed, black Irish way. She had to remind herself of all the things she didn't want from him.

He gripped her shoulders, pecked both her cheeks, leaving a wake of cologne-scented air. The twelve years between them lay before her like a cliff. It was hard to believe he'd once admired her cunt. He ordered a double espresso and didn't remove his coat. "You look good," he said.

"I'm fat."

"Did I say that? I'd say luscious."

"I thought you left LA because you hated people obsessing about looks."

"Learn to take a compliment. They don't come easily in this city. Not like LA."

If nothing else he could teach her to be snarky. He wiped his spoon with a napkin, and it reminded her of so much about him, how fussy he was, how germ-phobic, girlish in the way he checked his reflection in storefront windows, tweezed stray hairs, spread lotion nightly on his face and neck.

Someone across the café was smiling goofily in his direction. He nodded back.

"Are you, like, a celebrity now?"

"Some people know me. I'm an actor, it goes with the territory."

He wasn't really famous, was he? She couldn't tell. He winced as she scooped more whipped cream, but she didn't care. He sipped his espresso. "I've missed you," he said. "I need more old souls in my life."

She was only crying because she knew him more than she knew anyone else in this city, and because he knew her, at least a little. He gazed into his tiny cup. The silence was good—she hated false comfort.

"I hope you really want it, because it isn't easy here," he said.

"It? What is *it?*" She knew, but she wanted to hear what he'd say.

"We're not getting back together. Just to be clear."

"Of course we aren't. I don't want that. That's not why I'm here."

"But you want something. Money? Advice?"

"I'm fine, Julian."

"If you say so."

"I thought we might be friends."

He nodded. "Hey, I got a part in a Scorcese film. Ten lines."

"That's good, I guess?"

"Martin Scorcese." He shook his head. "Only the best filmmaker alive."

He offered to show her his place, a sublet on East 11th, but she said no, citing a prior commitment, proud of herself for refusing.

Jane again? A melted Buddha at the edge of the platform. What the fuck! Couldn't they find anyone else in this city of eight or nine million? Tasha wanted to draw a stranger, any stranger, not this person whose name she knew and whose ugliness had staked out a claim of moral superiority. Couldn't they get a beautiful model once in a while—was there something *wrong* with beautiful? Even thinking this Tasha knew she was wrong, knew this was the very thing that would keep her from being a real artist.

She hesitated in the hallway, other students hurrying past while she rode the accordion of leaving versus staying. She was paying for this, but she couldn't stand to be stuck in the same room with Jane for another three hours. *I won't make a habit of this,* she said to herself, turning to leave. Rupert was following her in his shuffling slippers—just her ruined luck.

"I'd like a word with you."

He hadn't said much to her for a couple of weeks. The things he had said were no help at all. *Use the poles to create dynamism.* How was she supposed to put comments like that to use? For all the money she was paying he should tell her how to fix things. Maybe she should just give up since it was clear he thought she was hopeless.

He watched her now with the same assessing gaze he brought to her work. A quivering nose hair poked from one nostril. "You have potential, dear. But something is getting in your way."

Could she step mutely into the elevator and leave? The elevator opened, disgorging another posse of students who swished past. *Hey, Rupert,* they said, their voices more windy worship than words.

"Jane is a wonderful model and challenging to draw. When you can draw her well you will have accomplished a great deal. Perhaps you're too young to appreciate her."

"I can't do anything about my age."

"Are you committed to this work, dear?"

It didn't feel as if he was talking to her, but to someone generally like her who he'd never respect. "Yeah." Then more emphatically, "Yes."

"It's not a question of: *Today I am too tired. Today I am not in the mood.* It's a question of making this your life. You must hunger for it."

"I do hunger for it."

"Then go back in there and show me. By the way, it might interest you to know that Jane is a very accomplished woman. She has a PhD in art history. And she's a member of Mensa."

For the next three hours Tasha drew in a blind rage. She drew her own hand. She drew one of the other students, a dirty-blonde with acne-scarred skin. She drew the tall windows, and a section of the building across the street. She ignored Rupert when he stopped behind her. She didn't give a rip if the work was bad. She tried to ignore Jane too, but couldn't completely because Jane had a way of taking over an entire room, her body a roaring dare: *Understand I'm beautiful.* At the end of the class Tasha tore up what she'd done and stuffed it into recycling.

It was already dusk. The light was smudged piss-yellow. Her heart pulsed like a broken bike chain. A bald man in a long black overcoat passed her. All these men in stupid power-coats. His mouth gyrated in wild figure eights like a sprung-to-life gargoyle. You couldn't tell who was crazy. Any passerby could turn on you. You were an anonymous body on whom others would play out their weird shit.

She called him on a whim. He buzzed her up, said he'd leave the door ajar. The apartment was small, a studio. The window divided the gray twilight into dozens of black-framed squares. The TV was playing "Cake Boss."

Julian sprawled on a large bed by the window. Even from a distance she felt the mist of his black mood. Cake Boss and his cronies were circling one of their creations, a huge red sports car with a man at the wheel, all made of cake. She stood watching the screen, men discussing midlife crises.

"Hi," she finally said. Julian's arm jutted forward like a lance to mute the TV. "Cool place," she said.

"It's not going to happen." He spoke to the ceiling. "It hit me today. I'm not going to be The Man. Not even for a minute."

She dropped her stuff, went to the end of the bed and perched there. "How do you know? You're just beginning."

"I'm thirty-two years old, Tasha. I'm not exactly beginning." What could she say? "That woman Brenda called. They want me to read again. They already told me I was cast and now, apparently, I'm not. They found someone else. Someone better than me."

"They said that?"

"Educated guess. Fact #1: They cast me. Fact #2: They uncast me. Obviously they want someone else."

"Can they do that? Cast and uncast."

"They can do whatever they want."

"It's only ten lines."

"It's Martin Fucking Scorcese."

"You act like he's some god."

"To me he's a god."

"You could always sue."

"Get a grip. I'm not going to sue. That's the quickest way to blacklist yourself."

Julian's eyes were closed. His face had absorbed the gray light. He should be blacklisted, she thought. You don't ask for sympathy then thrust it back meanly.

"I'm leaving."

He opened his eyes. "Don't go. I'm sorry." He got up and came to her and held her shoulders and guided her back to the bed. She watched herself being led as if in a hovercraft. He knew certain things about her—like how her mother had taken a shit in her agent's office and how news of that went public, ruining Tasha's life—but the things he knew didn't add up to everything she was.

She lay on her back and made him do the work. He peeled her leggings off, his fingernails scoring her thighs. He struggled with her bra, finally ripped it. Theatrics as usual, though in the old days he'd been gentle. Now his big blurry need shrouded her. With each thrust of his pelvis she became more and more invisible. She wasn't aroused, but she became wet anyway, hating herself. Afterwards, he got up and went to the bathroom to clean himself off. He couldn't stand to be sticky. He came back to bed with a glass of water. She closed her eyes and ignored the sound of his gulping as well as she could.

Her eyes opened in a panic. He'd forgotten a rubber. But no, there it was in an ashtray on the bedside table, a withered mess.

"You don't know what this means to me, Taz," he said.

She walked for hours, the hammering concrete sending arrows of pain up her femurs. It was after midnight when she arrived back at the Roses'. Mrs. Rose heard her and came floating down the hallway in a long nightgown like some Victorian ghost. "Is that you, Tasha?"

"Yes."

"You're alright?"

"Yes."

They both hesitated, Tasha sensing Mrs. Rose had more to say. *Don't worry. You're not my mother.*

"Sleep well," Mrs. Rose said before drifting back down the hallway.

Tasha couldn't help thinking of her mother. Her mother, the consummate actress, would never wear such drab clothes.

She slept into the afternoon and woke after class had started. The apartment was empty. She'd been dreaming of Jane, vague images of Jane standing over her, telling her off. She couldn't stand to think of how badly Jane thought of her. She had to talk to Jane. Apologize. Get herself on a better footing. Talking to Jane seemed suddenly urgent, the key to her success or failure as an artist.

The class was on break when she arrived. She hovered behind the door frame, peeking in, not wanting Rupert to see her. The model wasn't Jane. It was another one of Rupert's weird finds, a freakishly tall woman with an athletic frame and hair clipped short as a terrier's. Or was it a man?

"Jane Flint or Jane Cohen?" said the woman in the office.

"There're two Janes?" said Tasha. "The one from Rupert's class. The—large one." The woman wrote a number on a yellow post-it: Jane Flint.

Tasha scooted down the Bowery through the current of pedestrians as fast as her short legs would go. She shuttled through Whole Foods to the café area. It was Jane's choice to meet here, this opulent palace of food. Bouquets of lacy greens, root vegetables Tasha had never heard of, bins of nuts and aromatic coffee, glazed and braided breads, slabs of meat pink as babies' tongues, fish so fresh their glinting eyes seemed not to have registered their deadness. Everything perfectly stacked and artfully lit.

Jane had drawn up her motorized chair to a table at the back of the café, near a cooler of cheeses. Her eyes fell on Tasha. No turning back now.

Tasha stood over the tiny metal table, exposed as a beggar.

"Hi."

"I thought it would be you."

"I'm Tasha. From Mr. Pimble's class."

"I know who you are, gringa. Jane Flint here. But you know that—you called me. Get yourself something to drink."

42

Fat

"I'm fine."

"Suit yourself."

Jane sipped her coffee. The cup looked tiny. A piece of gray lint had lodged in the folds of her wrist. Tasha turned away, eyes landing on the wheels of orange and yellow cheese. She turned back again and scraped out the metal chair to sit.

"Well?" Jane said. "You asked me here."

The people at the adjacent tables were immersed in books or phones, firmly situated in the business of being their unique selves, but they would surely hear anything Tasha said.

"This isn't the best place to talk."

"You can't look at me, can you?"

Looking at Jane was dangerous as staring straight into the sun.

"You think I'm a freak."

"No, I—"

"You'll never be an artist if you can't look at people directly."

Jane was beginning to sound like Rupert. Tasha made a concerted effort. The light from the cheese case illuminated a caterpillar fuzz on Jane's upper lip. "I know."

"You know, but you don't really know. You want to be great, right? Famous? Make a lot of money with your art?"

"That's not—"

"But you're worried you'll fuck up somehow and end up like me. Confined to a chair."

Jane was getting worked up. She was short of breath. She took an inhaler from a bag that hung on the arm of her chair. Covering her nose and mouth with the device, she took a few deep breaths. Tasha imagined this must be how it felt to attend church and sit in a pew near the front, guilty of recent sin and being castigated by a minister who saw it all.

"You don't know anything about me," Tasha said.

Jane's laugh was husky. She raised both arms so her gauzy

purple over-blouse filled with air and her wingspan became wide as a condor's, startling a woman behind her who, scoping out cheese, took a quick step back. "Heavens," the woman said.

Jane shook her head. "Too many tight sphincters in this place." The woman scuttled away. "You live in a body like mine and you don't exist for most people. You're invisible. The plus is you get to observe what most people don't see. You wouldn't believe the things people do in public when they don't realize they're being watched." Tasha nodded.

"I used to be a court reporter. I saw so much shit in the courtroom I decided to make myself more useful. I'm back in school now to be a counselor."

"Wow."

"You didn't take me for a student, did you?"

Tasha shrugged. Was Rupert right about the PhD in art history? About Mensa?

"You tracked me down. But you haven't said why."

She was losing the thread of her purpose in being here. She closed her eyes. As always it was hard to get things straight in Jane's presence. "I'm really . . . I had a dream and you. . . ."

"Yes?"

"It's hard to explain." Her phone was vibrating loudly against the table's metal. Julian. *Fuck.* She silenced it.

"Well—?" Jane prompted.

"Nothing. An old boyfriend." She made a face.

Jane smiled. "Who did you wrong?"

"You could say that. He mauled me recently."

Jane reached out and placed her broad hand on top of Tasha's. Heat traveled with liquid speed up Tasha's forearm. "You didn't report it, did you?"

"It's not what you're thinking. It was my fault."

"It's an ordeal, no matter how you cut it."

Fat

Jane withdrew her hand and reached into her bag and found her wallet from which she extracted a small laminated photo that she handed to Tasha. An elfin girl of four or five with a riot of blonde curls, standing on a beach in a skirted red bathing suit. She held a plastic bucket and shovel, her legs were splayed. "Me at the Jersey shore."

Tasha was afraid of speaking.

"One of the many people I've been."

"You were adorable," Tasha said, immediately regretting her use of the past tense.

Jane ejected a laugh. "Yeah. Unfortunately two of my uncles thought so too."

Julian had called three times, left two messages. What the fuck did he want? Her ear? Her shoulder? Her cunt? Not now, not again. Certain mistakes you only make once.

She bought herself some new shoes, blue with tough soles, surprisingly hip. She shouldn't be spending money, but she'd have a job soon.

The Roses were out. She put on the shoes and wandered around the apartment, listening to the soles thunking over the floorboards. She peered into the rooms she'd never seen before, the master bedroom and a small study. They were orderly rooms and Midwestern-looking, with knock-off Colonial furniture, hooked rugs, lace curtains, not how she'd expected New York rooms to look. The queen bed was neatly made with a mauve quilt; on the dresser was the picture of someone she assumed was their son. She could have gone in, but she didn't. She'd been known to snoop, but her curiosity about the Roses was shallow and her thoughts were on Jane, the elfin child she'd been, the court reporter, the art historian.

Back in her room she listened to Julian's messages. It wasn't what she expected. He'd gotten the Scorcese part after all, and when he was in his agent's office he'd overheard people talking about her mother. In January she was going to be in an Off-Broadway production of *Who's Afraid of Virginia Woolf.* The agents were laughing about it. What if she took a shit right there on stage, wouldn't that be taking Martha to a new level! *Thought you'd want to know,* Julian's message said.

Tasha took off the shoes and turned them over to examine their soles. She sniffed the leather, put them on again. Her feet felt safe inside the shoes, her ankles strong. Off Broadway in January, rehearsals would probably start soon. Was she moving here to be close to Tasha, or because she'd made a fool of herself in LA?

The students were ready, easels set with pads of paper, extra charcoal sticks perched on their ledges. Midday sunlight sparkled down from the tops of the tall windows. *It's time to make art,* said the air's hush.

But the model was late. Ten minutes went by, fifteen. A tickertape of restlessness chittered up. People checked their phones. A few began texting. Some whispered, which annoyed Rupert, who left the room. Tasha was more aware than ever of being an outsider.

When Rupert reappeared everyone shut up. "There has been a change in plans." His enunciation was clipped. "Our model can't make it. I'd like a volunteer."

Embarrassed laughter tripped through the room. *You can't be serious.* People shook their heads, grinning. *No way, not me.* Rupert scanned the classroom slowly, considering the assets and willingness of each student. A clammy coldness clattered through Tasha. She understood what was about to happen. She was already moving to the platform by the time Rupert's gaze settled on her. "Yes," he said. "Good. Thank you, dear."

Fat

The room went silent but for the drone of traffic and some rattle in the heating system. She, the outcast, was stepping up. Her cheeks blazed. Rupert met her at the center of the platform, leaning in to instruct her in a low voice. She remembered him talking to Jane this way. He suddenly seemed kind. He told Tasha to remove her clothing, perch on the stool, and find a position she could hold for a while.

"I'll be back."

He left the room abruptly and she felt abandoned, frightened, as if the other students, unsupervised, might lynch her. There were so many items of clothing to remove to reach the point of nakedness. It would have been easier if she'd had a robe to remove in one quick careless motion.

She began with her new blue shoes then wriggled out of her leggings. The zipper of her skirt stuck. Her nylon sweater was sassy with static. Though she was shivering, sweat dripped from her pits. She stood frozen in bra and underpants, crossing her arms over her large private breasts, fighting vertigo. Why did she volunteer for this, how stupid could she be? She looked over the heads of the students directly in front of her and blurred her eyes, making the world go kaflooey. She thought of Jane, imagined she *was* Jane, a person who would always be hidden under her mountain of fat, offering it up for viewing like a loud *fuck you*. Jane was whispering in her ear now: *Go girl*. Tasha unhooked her bra, shimmied her hips to slide off her underpants, let her clothes stay where they fell, and sidled to the stool.

The murmur of moving charcoal took over the room. Enshrined by the room's hush, Tasha turned inward to a self they would never see. Her bowels rumbled. An itch leapt like a fly up and down her back. Her breath became shallow. She thought of her butt, wide and dimpled, splayed wetly across the stool. Not as fat as Jane's butt, but fat enough.

47

VANISHING

Rupert was back in the room, declaring a break. He offered her his overcoat to use as a robe. It swallowed her completely, but the wool was scratchy. He brought her bottled water and a bag of potato chips, and she sat in the corner checking her phone, not daring to look at the other students though she was dying to see what they'd drawn. A text from Julian: *Don't be mad, Taz. I need you.*

As she returned to the platform she glimpsed one guy's drawing. She didn't recognize herself. The head had huge Dumbo ears, and tufts of hair stood up like antennae. He flipped to an empty page before she could see more.

For the next posture she sat on the floor. She thought it would be easier to stay still, but it wasn't. Her spine ached and one foot went numb. She was hyper-aware of each beat of her heart. Pain twittered beneath her rib cage and in her shoulders. She tried picturing herself doing athletic things she couldn't actually do—gymnastics, skiing, swimming the breast stroke—but it didn't help. To master stillness you needed techniques she didn't have, focus she didn't have, the concentration of a yogi. Now more than ever she wanted to talk to Jane.

She listened to Rupert making his rounds, discussing the way light hit and sculpted her contours. *Look at the cheek,* he said, *look at the shoulder.* As if her whole body had no real substance, was made only of light.

At five o'clock the twilight appeared dark, the tall windows black but for the streetlights. Rupert had turned on the overhead fluorescents, which tinged the students' faces with gray-green exhaustion. Tasha no longer cared how other people had drawn her, she only wanted to move.

Wearing Rupert's coat she ferried her clothes down the hall to the ladies' room to change. How good walking felt. She dressed in a stall, reveling in the privacy.

Rupert was waiting in the empty classroom. She gave him

Fat

his coat and he put it on then exchanged his skull cap for a fedora. Impatience rained from him. "I need to be off. Thank you for filling in. I'll see about getting you some compensation."

He regarded her so intently she looked down at herself to see if her clothes were on backwards. She was fine though her static-y sweater clung like cellophane. She wanted him to say more than thank you, to acknowledge the difficulty of what she'd been through. But she could feel he was trying to get rid of her. She shrugged herself into her cheap leather jacket.

"Jane was scheduled to be here today," he said. Tasha nodded. "But she had a heart attack on her way to class." What was he saying—was Jane dead? "They took her to Beth Israel. I'm going to see her now."

"Is she okay?"

Rupert was already heading out the door, lifting his feet with more conviction than usual as if to assert his own health. They were the only ones in the elevator. Rupert withdrew to the corner, his big-nosed face channeling disaster. Tasha's unruly art pad thwacked the wall. The elevator churned to the ground floor.

"Can I come with you?" Tasha said as Rupert thrust out his arm to hail a cab.

"This isn't spectator sport. This is serious business." His kindness had evaporated.

"I know that."

The cab shot off without her. She idled on the corner, riddled with anger. Rupert hated her, that was obvious. Would he take her more seriously if she were disabled like Jane? He didn't *own* Jane.

Tasha's anger had dimmed a little by the time a taxi dumped her in front of Beth Israel. She left her drawing tablet in the cab on purpose. She would feel like a fool dragging it into a hospital.

VANISHING

Intensive Care, said the woman at the front desk. *Fourth floor.* Intensive Care was like a secret society with pneumatic double doors and signs prohibiting cell phones and children. Tasha summoned her courage then brazened in. She found herself in an unadorned ante-room with four chairs. Another set of double doors led to the ICU's main floor. A window offered a view of the nurses' station. She hesitated, then pushed through those doors too.

Curtained bays fanned out from the room's center. So much activity. Nurses bustling, machines beeping. Desperation swirled like smoke, so many fragile bodies struggling to maintain their grip. Living suddenly seemed like so much work.

"Jane Flint," she said to the nurse behind the counter.

The nurse checked her computer. "She has a visitor."

Rupert of course. "I have to wait?"

The nurse nodded. Tasha had never been in a hospital before and wasn't sure where to put herself. She returned to the ante-room and sat in a chair. Then she stood. Then she sat again. Each time she thought of Jane in a hospital bed she panicked. She needed Jane to be alive. She thought of the moment when she and Jane had said goodbye at Whole Foods. She bent down to hug Jane's warm stalwart body and felt linked to Jane in some way she wasn't linked to anyone else, either here in the city or back in LA. Rupert was taking so damn long.

There he was, blundering through the doors, doing a double-take when he saw her.

"You shouldn't be here," he said. "Jane is not a curiosity."

"Would I be here if I thought that?"

He pursed his thin lips. He looked like a gangster in his ridiculous coat. He was watching her as if his gaze alone could evict her. She should never have modeled for him.

Something drew her attention from Rupert, a summons curling up from Jane's damaged heart, spinning like a tornado out from behind Jane's curtained bed, past all the other patients, around the nurses' station, out the rasping doors to the flesh of Tasha's own beating heart. Jane wanted to see her.

"You don't own Jane," she said to Rupert.

Rupert closed his eyes as if to collect himself in the face of her childishness.

The curtain on Jane's bay was drawn back and its lights were fully lit. Jane's face and head were hidden by the rise of her body pushing the sheet into a monument. Tasha ducked past the thicket of tubes and IV bags to position herself at the side of the bed. Jane's face was splotched red and yellowish-white; her closed lids and lips were purple; her bloated arm lay on top of the sheet, taped with an IV tube. On the other side of the bed a machine beeped out her cardiac status.

"Jane?" Tasha whispered. The word scurried off. "It's me, Tasha. Are you all right?" She fixated on the broad forehead which took up most of Jane's face, picturing the massive brain behind it. "Jane?"

Jane remained still. Her breathing was too shallow to see. The heart machine nattered on. Tasha's attention was snagged by a stuffed bear with a red bowtie on the rolling trolley next to the bed. His cutesy smile was infuriating.

Something happened. A shift. Oozing from the still flesh, a defiant *Jane-ness* rose and filled the air. A palpable field of energy like heat, but not heat. It surrounded Tasha in a feeling of home. Jane was magnificent. She had probably descended from a long line of Pharaohs and queens.

The body began to move, almost imperceptibly. Tasha held her breath, a witness to Jane's returning consciousness. It was like watching a person being rebuilt. A swarming in her cheeks. A cluck in her throat. Tasha would later remember thinking: *This is joy.* Now she was impatient. *Open your eyes, Jane. Give me your full attention. There are so many conversations we need to have!* She wanted to tell Jane about modeling today, the way her skin had tingled and itched, about the geyser of uncontrollable restlessness. *And you?*

Jane's eyelids flickered and Tasha's own eyes, swimming in moisture, mirrored back the flickering. Tasha would recount this moment to Jane over and over in the months to come. *The moment you revived.* Tasha leaned down and, in a moment of spontaneous worship, planted a kiss on Jane's flannel cheek. Jane's arm shimmied. She spread her fingers. Her eyes opened.

"Hey," Tasha said. She saw the spark in Jane's irises, like cigarette tips on a dark football field attesting to the presence of human life.

Jane's lips parted. "Heh."

"Don't talk," Tasha said, though she was dying to hear what Jane had to say. She kept her gaze on Jane's beautiful monolith of a face and messages traveled back and forth between them.

A guttural croak. Feral panting. Fluid everywhere. The regular beep was now a keening alarm. Tasha called out.

People rushed in and surrounded Jane. They bludgeoned her chest with flat blocks. Tasha remained there until a nurse pushed her away and closed the curtain. Tasha didn't leave. She peered through the slit in the curtain, still holding the thread, still sending messages. Jane was there at the far end of the thread, lobbing messages back.

A grim-faced man sawed Jane's chest. This had to be a joke. He looked no more skilled than a carpenter. His tool looked crude. Blood flew everywhere, as if Jane had exploded. The man reached into Jane's chest. He cradled her heart.

Tasha gripped her end of the thread. It was all a matter of seeing, and now she saw Jane so very clearly.

VANISHING

Betsy Wainwright's brain was shrinking. Had shrunk. There was no certain diagnosis, only an objectively shrinking brain, measurably smaller in circumference this year than last. *Come and celebrate her fifty-first*, Betsy's husband Dan had said to Marty over the phone, at once jaunty and begging. *You're more likely than anyone else to dislodge some of her memories. And bring some of your finest California snake oil.*

Marty, newly single, was free to go wherever she wanted. But Dan's call brought her up short, shamed her. There was no denying she'd been neglecting her oldest friend who she hadn't seen for over three years, since before the brain's shrinking was identified. The length of her friendship with Betsy made it impossible to say no. They'd been three-year-old nursery school rug rats together and, though they'd always had different tastes and led very different lives and often lived for long stretches on different coasts without seeing each other for several years, the hours they'd logged in each other's company before they were twenty-two had made them almost siblings, and the relationship had hung on where others might have withered. It had the indestructability of a gnarled tree root that eventually becomes a fossil. Despite Betsy's difficulty, she was thrilling and larger-than-life, and being in her presence had always made Marty feel her own life was larger too. *You're a good egg,* they used to tell each other, out of the blue. Marty needed now, more than ever, to feel the possibility of a large life, a large life in which she could still be a good egg and not the self-absorbed person she'd become since her separation.

It was cold when she set out for New Hampshire from her mother's house in Massachusetts, and the sky was a monochrome sheet of gray, already churning out tiny flakes. Marty drove her tinny rental car slowly, performing her special trick: rearranging the focal distance of her eyes to see foreground and background simultaneously. It was the trick of one who had made a profession of squinting into a lens, a trick of her eyes, but more importantly a trick of the brain.

Betsy, Dan had reported, was no longer allowed to drive. If she drove, she lost her way. Once she'd arrived at the grocery store, and locked herself in her car, and couldn't figure out how to get out. This kind of dysfunction was alarming on so many levels that Marty usually tried not to think of it. Research had revealed that people were more likely to die not only soon after their spouses died, but also when others in their social circles died. What if losing brain capacity was the same way? Betsy's brain held memories of Marty's childhood that no one else shared. Betsy's vanishing memory was like losing a hard drive built over decades, one to which Marty was also wired.

In dwindling light Marty made her way slowly north through the surface streets to the highway, sucked inside a loop of tests. Should she remember this pink office building? This intersection? This Trader Joe's? It was true she hadn't lived here for years, but looking too hard at anything made it recede further from memory. The radio was broadcasting an interview with a thirteen-year-old violinist who would be playing a concer-

Vanishing

to with the Boston Symphony, written by a composer Marty had never heard of. The violinist, an uncannily precocious girl, spoke of the contrast between the movements, a challenging scherzo followed by a mournful adagio.

Two months ago Marty and her soon-to-be-ex-husband, Art, split their possessions down the middle—yours, mine, yours, mine—until they got to a stack of things no one wanted, objects shorn of meaning: a behemoth vegetable juicer they'd only used a handful of times, a set of ugly fuchsia bed sheets they had no recollection of buying, moth-eaten winter coats they'd had since their time in New York.

The day of their move to different apartments in Venice Beach they joked and laughed, the model of cooperation. She kept looking at Art's lanky body and his long artist's fingers, and wondering why they hadn't survived. They'd been such a good couple, he a painter until his recent foray into real estate, she a documentary filmmaker. They had great friends, gave lively parties, struggled together with their art.

At the end of that day Art got a call. It turned out he was going to France the following week. *You never said you were going to France*, she said. The look he gave her, a blank horizontal smile like a musical staff without notes, could have been read as pity. She understood she'd forfeited her right to indignation and stopped herself from asking who was going with him.

Twilight tipped into night and the snow intensified. The Ford Fiesta rattled and cold air seeped through a gap around the driver's side door. After years of living in California she was out of practice driving in snow and should have demanded a sturdier car. The trucks on all sides of her were equipped with chains, and plows had come out, appearing in her rear view mirror like prehistoric beasts, making a terrible racket. The black asphalt had become a path of white whose edges blurred into sky and falling snow, and occasional gusts of wind slung snow across the windshield, confusing her sense of up and down. She missed Art, the authority of his tall body. When they went on trips together he always drove.

Betsy Wainwright was also tall—over six feet—and bossy. She was almost beautiful—pictures preserved her that way—but in movement she became unsure of herself, gawky and blustery. Her family, Boston Brahmins with money, lived on a hill with a pond and horses, surrounded by pasture and woods. Her father was a writer and editor-in-chief, known in town and well beyond, a famous man himself who hosted famous authors for dinner. Sometimes Marty sat at those dinners, cowed by the erudite conversation about books and politics, nervous someone would ask her a question, uncertain how to serve herself gracefully from the dishes offered on the left by the maid. She always hoped Betsy would find a way to get them excused early.

But being excused had its own perils. Betsy often led her down to the pasture where they would ride the horse and pony bareback. This terrified Marty though she never said so. If you were timid, and prone to accommodating, and small as Marty was back then, it was only natural to go along with things. Bucky, the pony with the inauspicious name, was the one Marty was always instructed to ride. She clung to the bristly mane and held her breath as Bucky cantered after Betsy's horse, Simba. There was no slowing Bucky down, no convincing him he need not keep up with his longer-legged friend. For Marty there was only enduring. Her rump bumped over the pony's bony back like a pinball. She dreaded falling off, so easily could have. Betsy had stories of the horse girls around town "cracking their heads open." She would report this as if it was funny, and Marty envisioned a skull fractured like watermelon rind, a cross-sectioned brain spilled out and bleeding into the grass.

The car began to fishtail. She cast off her gloves to gain

Vanishing

more control of the wheel and steered into the skids. Her eyes telescoped toward the road, but the traffic had thinned and with no cars nearby there seemed to be no road at all, so she felt as if she was bombing forward on a pathless journey like those charted through space.

Her eyes pressed the white-dark for information, road signs, lights of towns, some confirmation she was on the right course. A mastodon lumbered into view then cartwheeled into an amoeba. A donkey lay out there, heaving in pain, spindly legs twitching. The whapping of tires against snow was indistinguishable from her own rough breathing. For god's sake, Martha, it's not a donkey, only a thin strand of unbidden memory.

Betsy's and Marty's lives took radically different directions sometime after college. Betsy, after a few dalliances, married Dan and got busy taking refuge from the world, building a house resembling her parents' house and raising their two children, Justin and Helen, on the hill in the New Hampshire countryside where Marty was now headed. Betsy had been on that hill for over twenty years. Was it possible, Marty now wondered, that Betsy had withdrawn from the world because her brain already, way back then, told her it was shrinking?

Marty, during that time, was throwing herself at the world. Ambitious (Betsy used to kid her about that), she went to graduate school, studied film, moved West, fashioned herself into a filmmaker. *Movies? Eee-gads!* Betsy had said when she learned of Marty's interest in film. Betsy, like her family, had always spurned popular culture—movies, TV, rock and roll, all brainless entertainment aimed at the low-level tastes of The Great American Public. *It's not Hollywood,* Marty explained of her film portraits of immigrant women. *It's documentary.* But it was all the same to Betsy, and by then Marty was able to slough Betsy's mocking. Despite her native timidity, Marty often said to herself about her own choices, especially recently, that she had gone out and faced the world, put herself into the fray. Maybe she didn't have a lot to show for it, maybe she had lost more than she'd won, but she couldn't be accused of shying away. She and Art had met and married in their early thirties. Neither wanted kids—who needed all that time chained to the house, all those trips to the ER to extract wasabi peas from noses. At some point Marty and Betsy, both good eggs, began to laugh companionably about their differences.

Still, Marty would always remember the times when Betsy's view of the world had to prevail. Once, in junior high, they biked on a Saturday morning to the school science fair. By the time they arrived Marty wasn't feeling well. *I think I'm going to be sick,* she told Betsy. *Oh, you're not sick,* Betsy said, turning and striding quickly inside while Marty vomited on the stairs just outside the front door, so everyone coming and going saw.

Or the trip to Yosemite. It was during or after college, she couldn't quite remember. Betsy and Dan were together, but weren't yet married. Marty had flown from New York to Santa Cruz where Betsy and Dan were living at the time, and they had driven to Yosemite to cross-country ski. But it had been raining and they spent the better part of a day driving around in search of a place with snow from which to embark. Finally they settled on a trail that led them through the flat-lands over sticky snow, trees dripping overhead, skis scratching exposed rocks and twigs, nothing vaguely majestic about the scenery. Eventually they took off their skis and carried them, like unruly chopsticks, back to the car, arriving just before another downpour.

They were renting a one-room cabin. The wood was so wet the fire hissed and sent out rank black smoke, so they gave up on the day, and warmed some soup, and went to bed in two double beds, only a foot apart. Marty lay stiffly with all her clothes on. She wasn't modest exactly, but she felt strange bedding down so close to a couple who might want to have sex. She

Vanishing

stayed as still as she could, feigning sleep. Betsy and Dan began to whisper, quietly at first, then more loudly, until it was clear they were both furious. Now Marty really didn't dare move. She was sure the argument was her fault. She strained to hear, but only single words and phrases were decipherable: *should have told me, never said that, there, here, wasn't, couldn't, she.*

It was her birthday, Marty now recalled, along with her recent college graduation that had been the occasion for the California trip. Betsy had made her a cake and threw a party though none of the guests were people Marty knew. The next day Dan took them to a strip tease show, saying it was an important Life Passage. Being from California he thought of himself as more worldly than his New England upper crust girlfriend, definitely more racy. Despite Betsy's resistance, the three of them drove into San Francisco where, at a club they watched a woman in a G-string draping herself gymnastically over various parts of a grand piano. She touched herself suggestively and did splits and backbends and walkovers as her inky hair rained over breasts and buttocks. Marty and Betsy were the only women there, and the other men were all a lot older than Dan, not sleazy-looking exactly, but people Marty preferred not to look at for too long. She tried to be game and smiled aggressively. Dan's attention cycled from the performing woman to Betsy to Marty. He looked mischievous, enjoying the shock he was inflicting on the woman who would become his wife, and her friend, both too prudish. At some point Betsy began to laugh, a low gravelly ooze of laughter that lasted a full minute before she got up and escaped to the lobby. Dan raised an eyebrow at Marty. *Shall I go out?* she asked. *She's fine,* Dan assured her. *She'll get over it.* But Betsy never returned, and Marty and Dan watched for the next forty-five minutes alone.

It was after midnight when she arrived at the bottom of the

driveway. It was a miracle she'd arrived at all. Several inches of snow had fallen since the road's last plowing, and the steep quarter-mile driveway had not been plowed at all and hosted over a foot of snow. She wedged her car into a snow bank to get it off the road, tossed a few clothes and toiletries into her carryon backpack, and plunged forward, uphill, keeping her eyes on the outdoor light Dan had left on. The snow came almost to her knees and wormed over the tops of her boots. If she hadn't been so tired it would have been gorgeous, the snow untouched, the moon almost full, a few light flurries pirouetting in and out of the light like fairy dust. She and Betsy had a name for glittering snow, a long multi-syllable name that was hard to recall now. *Triglick*—something. The thought of bed kept her going. In the old days Betsy would have made sure there was a hot water bottle between the sheets, cocoa on the night stand. *Drink the damn cocoa,* she would order Marty who, as a child, never liked hot drinks. She passed a small barn. Only a shed really. So much about this place was an exact replica of what Betsy had grown up with. Marty's own life bore not a shred in common with the lives of her parents.

Someone had shoveled an area by the side door. Huffing, Marty entered the mudroom, picking a path through a hodgepodge of shoes and boots, jackets and mittens fallen from their pegs. She stumbled into the foyer. Something was different, she felt it immediately. A strong smell of mustiness and old food and something acidic. It reminded her of the lobby of the first building in New York where she and Art had lived together. They speculated about that smell endlessly, trying to dissect it, deciding it emanated directly from the walls and ceiling and floor of the building itself. It wasn't decay, but a precursor to decay.

Though the light was dim she could already feel that things were not tidy. In the morning, when snow-reflected light would invade every room, she would see the untidiness she now only

Vanishing

felt. Books pulled from shelves, pieces of mail here and there, pots and pans scattered around the living room, glitter winking up from the hardwood floors like Hansel and Gretel crumbs though far less deliberate. What she gleaned now in the shadows, illuminated only by a night light down the hall, was a kind of shabbiness. *WELCOME*, said a note on the floor. *Glad you made it. First bedroom on the right upstairs. Excuse the mess. Dan.*

She wasn't quite ready for sleep. Her shoulders were tense, and she felt as if she was still gripping the steering wheel. She set her backpack at the bottom of the stairs and went to the kitchen for milk. It had been hours since she'd eaten. By instinct she found the cookie canister, which in Betsy's households had always been filled with homemade cookies. It was the same resilient green canister with the painted rose that Marty remembered from Betsy's childhood home. Remarkable, the things that lasted. She wasn't surprised to find the canister empty, a couple of stale Oreos at the bottom. She ate them both and washed them down with milk then stood at the sink which offered a view of the living room and its large picture window that looked out on a hazy moon and a sloping snow-covered field. During the day there would be a distant view of the valley. She drank in the peace, understanding why Betsy had always loved it here.

A mouse-like rustling. It was Betsy, she now saw, right in her eyeline, sitting in an easy chair in the living room, back to Marty, stroking the chair's arm and staring out. Even the shadowed silhouette of her cheek and shoulder were immediately recognizable. Had she been there all along, since Marty came in? Marty vacillated. She didn't have the energy to interact with anyone right now, let alone the uncertain persona Betsy promised to be. And if she announced herself Betsy might think she was an intruder. But could she get upstairs without being heard? Should she wake Dan and tell him Betsy was down here? Betsy thumped the chair's arm in a regular rhythm. Was this a communication, Betsy to Marty? Holding her breath, Marty tiptoed back into the hallway, retrieved her backpack, and headed upstairs. At the top of the stairs the thumping stopped.

The sound of a snow blower awakened Marty. It was late, almost 9:00. From the bedroom window she could see Justin, tall like his father and mother, clearing the driveway. The day was blue and white, resplendent, the entire hillside covered with a puffy duvet of snow.

Downstairs in the kitchen Dan and Helen greeted Marty with expressive hugs as if they were squeezing away the years since they'd seen each other. The three-plus years had aged Dan; his unruly hair was longer and grayer, and he sported a small paunch. In the four or five years since Marty had seen Helen, Helen had bloomed from girl to woman. Dan was making another pot of coffee. He was his usual lighthearted, talkative self. He'd made peace with his lot here as a one-size-fits-all country attorney.

"You certainly are intrepid," Dan said. "Was the driving awful? It somehow doesn't seem right that you ended up on my sunny coast, and I'm stuck here in your land of polar vortexes. Your mother is well?"

"Same as always."

Helen thumbed through cookbooks. She was robust and forthright, up for the weekend from Boston where she had just begun law school. In appearance she took after Betsy, though she was much more of the current world.

"It's just us tonight," Helen said. "The family and you. Too many people doesn't work with Ma. We're keeping it simple— chicken, rice, broccoli, cake. We *have* to have cake. It's not good for her, but what's a birthday without cake."

Vanishing

Dan poured mugs of coffee and the three sat at the nicked farmhouse-style table, Dan and Helen regarding Marty expectantly. "Well, what's the news from California?" Dan said.

"Same old. Still making films no one will see. Still teaching to pay the bills."

"Sorry to hear about you and Art. Although that's what you get for going to Hollywood."

Marty laughed. "Me and Hollywood, we're very tight. How's your practice?"

"Fine, when my clients aren't killing each other and practicing incest."

"I guess your father's optimism about the law is what convinced you to go to law school?"

"A means to an end," Helen said. "I wouldn't recommend it. I'm sure making films is a lot more fun."

"Sometimes. Where's Betsy?"

"She sleeps late," Dan said. "She often gets up in the night and wanders."

"Is that safe?"

Dan shrugged. "You're not one of those people who believes life is risk-free, are you? She manages. Better sometimes than others."

Helen rolled her eyes. "I keep telling Dad—"

"That I'm hopeless. That I should hire someone to look after her. Or put her somewhere. But honestly, wouldn't you want to be free and unsupervised as long as you could be?"

"Free to kill yourself in any number of ways."

"She's not going to kill herself. It's only mishaps."

"So far." Helen turned to Marty. "I've offered to quit law school. At least for a while until we can find someone else."

"There's no need to quit school. You've got your things to do. Your mother has hers."

Helen's chair scraped the linoleum. She stood and gulped

the dregs of her coffee. "Let's go wake her up. Come on, Marty. You know the protocol?"

"Move slowly. Get her attention before speaking."

Helen nodded. "Calm, but no condescension. She isn't a child though you wouldn't know it sometimes."

They headed upstairs, leaving Dan in the kitchen. Helen smoldered. "He's impossible. He doesn't realize how far gone she is. Oh sure, sometimes she's perfectly logical and coherent, but not for long. I can't figure out if he's naïve or just stupid."

"I've never thought of him as stupid."

"Not on paper, no, but sometimes he's amazingly functionally impaired."

Outside Betsy's closed bedroom door Helen stopped and considered Marty. "I can't believe how long you two have been friends. I honestly can't imagine knowing anyone for so long."

Helen opened the door on a room that was not the master bedroom. It appeared to be a playroom of sorts, with shelves of plastic horses and ponies, stuffed animals of all sizes, beanie babies, blue and purple yoga balls. One wall was decorated with cutouts of stars and moons, the opposite wall with fish.

"I know, I know," Helen whispered as Marty surveyed the room. "Dad got her all these things. For a while it was his big project. Actually, she kind of likes it, especially the soft stuff."

Marty nodded, suddenly apprehensive. In a four-poster bed loaded with quilts Betsy slept, only a few strands of her graying blonde hair visible.

"Mum—" Helen rattled Betsy's shoulder.

"Don't wake her on my account."

"We have to keep her on a somewhat normal schedule. Ma, wake up. Someone is here to see you."

Betsy grunted, turned over, and rose slowly to a sitting position. She regarded her daughter, expression slack.

"Ma, it's me, Helen." Helen's face was no more than a foot

Vanishing

from Betsy's. Betsy grinned suddenly, and reached out for a hug. "It's your birthday, Ma. Happy Birthday."

Betsy was now all business. She threw back the covers and burst out of bed.

"You go pee and I'll come help you get dressed." Helen yanked off the sheets. "She peed. She often does."

Marty didn't need to be told, the smell permeated the room. Seeing Marty, Betsy stopped. They latched gazes. Something swam at the back of Betsy's cornflower eyes, translucent as streambeds, the same as ever. Helen hurried over.

"This is your old friend, Marty. She came from California for your birthday." Helen spoke as if pressing the words past layers of something viscous.

"Hi, Betsy," Marty said. She smiled hard, focused on the eyes, the familiar eyes, trying to ignore the rest, the blank look, the hay-dry hair, the cracked lips, the stench, the sudden awkward intimacy. Betsy's lips quivered, as if she was about to speak.

"Happy Birthday," Marty said. She waited.

"Happy Birthday," Betsy echoed. "Happy Birthday." Her smile was jubilant. She lunged forward, throwing the full weight of her large body into Marty, nearly knocking Marty down. "Martha," she said into Marty's hair and neck. Her grip was fierce, her arms and back bony but strong.

Marty laughed. They pulled back and laughed together. Marty was filled with an unexpected surge of elation. "You're the only person in the world who still calls me Martha."

Martha went downstairs while Helen helped Betsy dress. Dan was playing the piano, a baby grand set in a book-lined alcove of the living room. He pounded out a jaunty Scott Joplin tune that matched his personality. Justin looked up from his computer. He had the cheerful unflappability of his father. Marty took a seat beside him on the couch. A white cat with long hair and green eyes leapt into her lap.

"I didn't know you had cats."

"We didn't until recently. Seamus, our very old dog, died, and a neighbor brought us this cat, thinking we needed another animal. Ma fell in love with him before Dad could say no."

"What's his name? Or hers?"

"We call him Albert, but Ma has a million names for him. Whatever seems right at the moment."

"Your mother was never a cat person. She always preferred dogs. And horses."

Justin laughs. "I think she's a lot of things now she never was before. How are they doing up there?"

"Fine, I think."

"Helen isn't always the most patient."

"She seemed okay to me."

"Just wait. It's weird, you know—the whole thing."

After a lot of restless movement, Albert settled, and Marty stroked his back. "She remembered me, your mother did."

"You sound surprised."

"I wasn't sure what to expect."

"It comes and goes. Dad keeps thinking something is going to jiggle everything back into place. But that's pretty much magical thinking."

"How does he manage when you two aren't around?"

"Neighbors with hearts of gold. It won't last forever. We're trying to nudge Dad into making other arrangements. Or in Helen's case, bulldoze him."

The deep snow, the blinding sunlight, the family gathered, the birthday, the guest—there was a cast to the day that set it apart, removing them all from the surly march of time. Martha, who was no longer Marty, tried to stay centered in the day's peace, its lack of pressing demands, but something thrummed on. Perhaps it was only the frayed nerves of the traveler, or the recently uncoupled. She wasn't used to being in the midst of another family. The past spirited around them like smoke. She missed Art, kept picturing him walking on the beach with a woman, the faceless nameless one she imagined he'd taken to France. She knew Art wasn't thinking of her. He hadn't called her once since the separation, and she felt gone to him, along with all those years they'd spent together. Poof.

Before she left California she had made an effort to dig into unpacked boxes and find a few photographs, mostly small black-and-white snapshots taken years ago with a Brownie camera. She laid them out on the coffee table. There was a tattered school photo of Betsy in sixth grade looking angelic in a white blouse, smiling expansively to expose her dimples. There was one of her astride Simba, her downturned gaze fond as he reached his neck forward to graze on something tasty. There was another of her as an early teenager leaping, suspended mid-air, mid-laugh, scarf of hair rippling behind her. Despite the photograph's lack of focus, the joy could not have been clearer.

Everyone leaned in to look, everyone except Betsy who sat on the carpet nuzzling her face into Albert's fur.

"Pictures of you, Ma," Justin said. "When you were younger. Want to see?"

Betsy ignored him, or didn't hear. Martha got up and sat beside Betsy on the carpet. She reached out to pet the cat. Betsy's head shot up, eyes like road flares. *This cat is mine.* Martha withdrew her hand.

"You were so beautiful, Ma," Helen said.

"A heartbreaker," Dan said. "Why else do you think I married her? Not to mention that she rescued me from my ignorance and squalor."

Helen placed the photo of Betsy leaping into Betsy's hand. "Look. That's you."

Betsy looked. She smiled but said nothing. Did she recognize herself? She handed it back.

Sunlight reflecting off the snow invaded the house, bleaching everything, exposing layers of dust almost congealed into felt. Betsy's attention flew here and there like a gnat, erasing Martha one moment, then bringing her back to life.

Helen shooed them out of the house for a walk—*Ma needs her walk*—while she stayed behind to bake the cake. It was so bright out Martha could scarcely open her eyes. She had left her sunglasses in California not imagining she would need them Back East at this time of year. She and Art always used to talk about light: how to capture it on canvas, how best to deploy it in film, what bright and low light did to the shapes of faces.

Betsy stood on the compacted snow of the driveway, staring down at her booted feet.

"Is she up to this?" Martha asked Dan quietly.

"Oh, she's fitter than all of us, aren't you Bets? On a day with no snow she walks for miles."

Martha eased up to Betsy, offered an arm. Wordlessly Betsy linked. The moment of wariness in the living room had passed. The four began to advance slowly down the driveway. Betsy was still as strong as she'd always been, but she placed each foot forward as if the ground's solidity was not to be trusted, as if gravity itself might be in flux. This mode of attack seemed right to Martha. She, too, was stepping cautiously. The driveway was slippery in places and with sunlight popping off so many surfaces, appearing unexpectedly through branches like flashing blades, it was hard to see things clearly.

Dan and Justin ambled ahead, side by side, occasionally pausing to look back, adjusting their pace. They were speaking of Justin's plans. He did computer consulting work which he could access from anywhere in the world, and next week he would be going to Italy to see his girlfriend. He could come back at a moment's notice, he told his father, he might even bring his girlfriend. "Don't worry," Dan assured him. "We're fine on this hill, just fine."

"Gadzooks!" Betsy said out of the blue.

Martha laughed. *Gadzooks*—quintessential Betsy.

"Gadzooks!" Martha repeated.

"Everything is cattywumpus." Another Betsy word. Betsy stopped walking and brought her face close, so Martha could feel her moist breath. "Cattywumpus!" Betsy was triumphant.

They both laughed, Betsy opening her mouth so wide Martha could almost see her tonsils.

"Cats," Betsy said, clamping her free mittened hand on Martha's arm. "Cats!"

"Cats, yes," Martha said, nodding hard.

"*Blurp, blurp, blurp*—not like we used to—we used to—didn't we?—we—"

Martha nodded uncertainly. A braying, loud and hoarse, came from the shed. "What the hell is that?"

"Horrible, isn't it?" Dan laughed. "It's a donkey."

"You have a donkey?" Martha said. "Why? You can't ride a donkey, can you?"

"Betsy loves donkeys, right Bets? If it were exclusively up to her we'd have more than one."

"Shall we tell her?" Justin said.

"Tell who what?" Martha said.

"The donkey's name is Martha."

"Oh, for god's sake. Should I be insulted or flattered?"

"Perhaps a bit of both," Dan said. "All in good fun, right."

"You know our donkey story, right? Betsy's and mine?"

"Oh, yes," Dan said.

"I don't," said Justin. "Tell me."

Martha glanced at Betsy whose face had settled back into

default slackness. "Later," Martha said. "Not now."

Inside the dim shed Betsy unhooked her arm from Martha's, straightened, so Martha saw her as a youth, imperious, beautiful, as yet unimpaired. The donkey, lusting for company, elongated her long neck over the gate, lifted and lowered her head as if nodding, cavernous mouth opening on ugly yellow teeth. Betsy hurled her arms around the ungainly animal, muttering and cooing. Dan caught Martha's eye then looked away.

The house was redolent with baking cake. *What now?* Martha thought. How would they fill this endless day? She admired a wall hanging in the foyer, a colorful folkloric tapestry depicting Noah's flood. "Beautiful," she murmured.

"You gave us that," Dan said. "Or you gave it to Betsy."

"I did?"

"Years ago. Before we were married. We've always had it hanging somewhere."

Martha touched the cloth, fondling one of the three-dimensional elephants, trying to remember. Where would she have gotten such an item? "I think you're thinking of someone else."

"I don't think so," Dan said. "We have all sorts of Martha detritus around here. It's my job to remember these things."

"Detritus?"

"Choose a better word—relic, memento?"

Did he remember Yosemite? Did he remember the strip club? She'd have liked to ask, but was loathe to resurrect anything difficult. Betsy's bare feet slapped the hard wood as she headed to the living room. Her bottom swayed under loose gray sweatpants. She wasn't fat, but everything about her had relaxed, become loose and acquiescent to gravity.

"Do you get lonely?" Martha asked Dan quietly.

Dan deflected the question with a grin.

"What should I do now?" She needed a task.

Vanishing

"Go with the flow. You're the Californian now, you should know about that. Maybe Helen needs some help."

But Helen refused help, the cords of her neck rippling, so Martha perched on the couch, tethered again to Betsy, though Betsy had settled on the carpet, devoting herself to Albert. Dan stood by the bookcases sorting through mail. Helen bustled in and out of the kitchen looking for birthday candles. Justin went upstairs and came down again with paper and scissors.

"Paper dolls," he said to Martha. "I've discovered I have a knack and Ma loves them. So tell me the donkey story." He began folding, fingers precise as he ironed each fold.

"It might be upsetting."

"Okay, then don't."

A colander, resting upside down on the floor by the picture window, toyed with the bright light. Betsy appeared to be elsewhere, communing with Albert, extending her tongue to touch his whiskers. Martha lowered her voice.

"We were on a pack trip with Betsy's parents. In the North Cascades. We were fourteen, Betsy and I. We rode the horses, Betsy and me and her parents and our guide Elmer. And the donkeys—well, mules really—were carrying our gear. And one day one of the mules fell while we were crossing a bridge, and he broke his leg, and Elmer had to shoot him. It shocked me. I'd never even *seen* a gun before. I can still picture that poor mule lying dead by the side of the trail."

Justin had stopped his snipping to listen. "Wow. No wonder Ma wanted a donkey."

Betsy leaned forward, focused as a striking rattler. Albert flew off her lap. "No. Elmer never shot the donkey." She shook her head violently so her hair darted out, spoke-like, in all directions. "No!" She was yelling now, utterly fluent. She slapped the coffee table. "That donkey was not shot."

Martha froze. Justin dropped his scissors, leapt to Betsy's

71

side, slung an arm around her back. "Everything's fine. No one's shot." His voice was low and smooth, a lullaby, a perfect anodyne. "The donkey is okay. She's down in her shed, very happy."

"Elmer never shot the donkey." Betsy clamped her teeth up and down. "Not shot."

"Not shot," Justin said. "Elmer did not shoot any donkey."

Betsy snared Martha with an implacable look, replete with all the old diminishing power she used to use to assert her world view. Martha felt like a criminal. Of course Elmer shot the donkey. She wouldn't have made that up. She turned away from Betsy's savage glare.

"I'm sorry," she said to Justin.

"It happens. I shouldn't have pushed you."

Betsy scrunched her face and wiggled her torso and flapped her hands around her ears as if to fend off an onslaught of flies. Martha rose and went upstairs and shut the door to her room and lay on the bed. She had always prided herself on her memory. Art had a terrible memory. He probably did not remember how they used to lie on the bed in her New York apartment, early in their courtship, and gaze down into the apartment across from them, a floor below. That bed, too, was near the window, and once, unable to wrench their gazes away, they watched the woman who lived there making love. For months after that they would see the woman in the building's lobby and feel ashamed. But Art wouldn't remember that now. She closed her eyes on the mote-filled light. How easily certain things were extinguished. And other things, the very ones you wanted so desperately to erase—Art's look of readiness and relief when she suggested they separate—were the very ones that clung so tenaciously.

She had read an article not long ago about a monk with a superlative memory. Over the course of a day people would bring him things—a shoe, a flower, an equation, a question—and at the end of the day he was able to remember in perfect sequence the five hundred things he'd been shown or told. His secret, he said, was meditation.

A nap gave her the strength to go down again. Justin had made multiple strings of paper dolls, and he and Betsy were on the couch bent over the coffee table, decorating the dolls with colored pencils. Justin was giving them faces and outfits, Betsy was applying indeterminate spidery lines. She looked focused, happy.

Martha sat at the far end of the couch. Betsy didn't acknowledge her. It fascinated Martha, this obliviousness. She almost envied Betsy. Fixated on drawing, she was immune to her dowdy appearance, unconcerned about having yelled so recently at Martha.

Dan stationed himself at the piano again. He played more quietly now, a Chopin piece from which he segued into familiar show tunes. The musical phrases wafted over Betsy's face. She put down her pencil, noticed Martha, and slid closer until they were shoulder-to-shoulder.

Dan sang now, quietly, his tenor surprisingly clear for a lawyer in his fifties. ". . . my honey lamb and I, sit alone and talk, and watch a hawk making lazy circles in the sky. . . ."

"You don't sing?" Martha asked Justin.

"God no. Ma sings sometimes, but Helen and I are just spectators. We never got that gene."

He handed his completed paper dolls to Betsy. She flattened them on her lap, swaying, body leashed to the music. Tentatively, Martha laid a hand on Betsy's lap. Betsy leaned in and rested her head on Martha's shoulder, and Martha's entire body filled like a cistern with deep animal satisfaction.

"Maria," Dan sang, "Maria, I just met a girl named Maria. . . ." He looked over at his audience with master-of-ceremony confidence, and nodded an invitation. "You know these words, Bets. Sing with me. Martha, come on, sing along."

Betsy's body shifted, trembled. She sat erect, lit by something, about to sing. "She's *my* friend. Not yours. Mine!" Her voice filled the living room, her gaze fixated on Dan.

Dan stopped playing.

Betsy clapped her palm on Martha's thigh, squeezed. "You can't do that with her. She's mine!"

Dan stared into his lap. Had he told her? Or had she sensed it? A single foolhardy moment years ago that no one wanted to repeat, meaningless and buried by decades, mostly forgotten. Why now?

"No one is doing anything with anyone," Dan said. "Right Martha?"

Martha's voice was not her own. Turning to Betsy she seemed to ventriloquize. "No, of course not. He wouldn't do that. Neither would I. I'm yours Betsy, not his. *Your* friend."

"What's going on?" Justin asked.

Dan waved his hand. "Nothing. Believe me."

Martha's face was inches from Betsy's. She stroked Betsy's red cheek with her forefinger. Its nerves seemed capable of receiving and transmitting everything that would ever be important. Betsy had answered a question Martha never knew she had.

"I'm yours," Martha said. Her hand trembled and so did her breath. "We're best friends. Right?"

Betsy's agitation began to subside. A smile poked forth, sun behind rain. "Are you a good egg?" Betsy said.

A good egg. Plucked from her gray matter's labyrinth of tangles and plaques. "Oh, god, yes," Martha said. "I'm a good egg. And so are you. You're a very good egg."

"I'm a good egg?"

"Yes. Of course. We're both good eggs."

Vanishing

"We're both good eggs."

Outside the sun, thinking about setting, was turning pink. A few chickadees pecked at the snow, hunting for what might be beneath. Helen had come in from the kitchen. The silence was strange, amorphous. Could anyone hold onto a self without the regard and memories of others?

"I think it's time for cake," Helen said.

"Isn't it a bit early?" Justin said. "Don't we usually have the cake at dinner?"

"It's time for cake now," Helen insisted. She disappeared and appeared moments later with a tiered chocolate cake, its top smeared with thin layer of pink icing, a single fat candle blazing at its center. "Play," Helen commanded.

Dan began to play. "Happy Birthday to you. . . ."

"Speed it up," Helen said. "That sounds funereal."

He did as Helen insisted. Martha didn't look at him, could not, kept her hand on Betsy's thigh. They sang together—*Happy Birthday to you, Happy Birthday to you*—every particle of history, shared and unshared, remembered and forgotten, floating by in the afternoon light, traveling to great distance, then inexplicably returning.

The song ended, but Betsy kept singing, "Happy Birthday, dear Betsy, Happy Birthday to you. To you. To you." Her palm slapped Martha's leg. "You. You."

Helen laid the cake on the coffee table, and Betsy stared at the flame, mesmerized, her face lit with disbelief and rapture. A moment of uncertainty billowed, filled the room. Then, as if on cue, Betsy and Martha leaned forward together and blew out the flame.

REDHEAD

On the morning of the celebration for Thomas's dead wife Isabel a chilly rain fell, unseasonal for late May, though these days who could bank on seasonal. Seeing the umbrellas and raincoats, the quick dashes for cover as the clan gathered, Morna was glad to be in her apartment, warm and snug, settling in for her first nicotine fix of the day. She scanned the crowd, wondering which one of them would be the next to die, casting her vote with a woman who stood at the edge of a small group, skittish and curiously alone. They might be genuinely sad down there, but from Morna's vantage point their appropriate little faces looked like bereavement emojis. Morna hadn't really been part of this clan since graduation, and she didn't wish to be part of it. They were sons and daughters of toney-brained parents: neurosurgeons and novelists, economists and astronauts, eco-entrepreneurs and bishops. "My dad's an insurance adjuster," Morna used to say when people asked in the early days of her freshman year. "And my mom's in HR." They gave her uncomfortable, vaguely scandalized looks, and the conversation would grind to a halt. By second semester she had a new story. Her mom was leading HIV education programs all over Africa.

Redhead

Her dad was a neuroscientist who delivered regular reports on the state of the post-millennial brain.

The rain began a new tirade, pelting the sidewalk, clearing the small crowd that had stopped to exchange condolences. Emptied of people, the courtyard berated her. She should have made alternative plans for the day, something to distract from the unfurling drama across the street which, though it held no more emotional juice for Morna than a back page news story, was impossible not to watch. It had been one of the gossip items circulating for the past few weeks among her former college classmates. Married before graduation, dead by twenty-five from a stage four something-or-other.

A person in a black trench coat darted across the courtyard, exited through the iron gate, and crossed the street. He went into the newsstand and a minute later retraced his path back to the church. Inside the gate he stopped. It was Thomas, standing in the downpour with his face to the sky, his famous ringlets soaked and punished into lifeless strands. He remained there for what seemed like a long time under the circumstances, knees bent as if he might collapse, trench coat no longer repellent under the sheer volume of rain.

She dressed in thirty seconds, grabbing the most available clothes—black skirt, black sweater, knee-high zippered black boots, her own black trench coat. In the elevator she swiped her lips with mauve lipstick. By the time she reached the churchyard, taking the short cut, splashing through puddles, Thomas was gone.

She entered the church tentatively. Would Thomas have chosen this church if he'd known she lived across the street? She'd only been here twice before, both times for dance concerts, both times thinking of it as a place both hip and historical more than religious, though it was true they held Sunday services every week. She stood at the back, behind a packed house, standing room only. For an event that had been billed as a celebration, the atmosphere was forbiddingly solemn. A male cellist seated on the stage in a pocket of celestial blue light played an adagio solo. Morna vaguely recognized the guy from college though she couldn't have said his name. He rocked back and forth with each stroke of his bow. Behind him a harpist awaited her turn in the shadows, head bowed. The Facebook announcement had encouraged people to bring offerings—artworks, poems, songs—it was so like Thomas to want to dress an event like this in the gauzy garb of art. He was a painter with flirtatious blue eyes that sometimes turned inexplicably inward, a low center of gravity, swarthy skin from his mother's Italian-American family, and hair that, when dry, fell past his jaw in Little Lord Fauntleroy ringlets. His congenial manner drew people in and hid his artistic ambition. Morna had gone out with Thomas herself at the beginning of junior year, but broke up with him after spring break in a preemptive strike, sensing he was about to break up with her. He'd been an intense lover, but spacey and inattentive, and after a while Morna had lost track of who she was with him.

She scanned the crowd, looking for a place to settle, trying to match the backs of necks and cant of shoulders with classmates she expected would be there. Christopher Johnston, Sarah Bernstein, Hope Finley.

Only a few feet from her Thomas leaned against the wall. He had shed his soggy trench coat in a heap on the floor, but his black shirt and pressed black pants were also drenched, and locks of his wet hair shed drops like leaky spigots. His body shocked Morna; it was so much scrawnier than when she'd known him, and his once-swarthy skin now exuded an unhealthy pallor. His torso quaked, and a filament of mucus hung from his nose, swinging like a broken spider web. She had never seen him cry before, and if she'd ever tried to imagine it

Redhead

she would have pictured eloquent, high-minded grief, a behavior abstract as dance, not this ghastly, snotty, quivery display.

He felt her stare and looked over, eyes unguarded, surprise and recognition bubbling up through his sorrow. Stumbling to her, he laid his wet head on her shoulder, compelling her to drop her umbrella and lay an arm around his back. "Oh Thomas, I'm so sorry," she whispered.

It was not possible that she had ever wished Isabel dead, that she had chanted to herself after learning of Thomas's imminent marriage—less than six months after her own breakup with him—*Iz is not.*

Everyone loved Isabel. Morna only knew her from afar; she would see her eating lunch at the Commons, sometimes swimming at the gym. She was a big woman, tall and soft-bodied, with Callipygian hips, long dark hair, and a languid, French-y manner that Morna thought pretentious. She dressed in skirts that played around her calves, and she pinned up her hair asymmetrically, fastening it with whatever twig or chopstick or bone was available. When Morna saw Isabel she was often laughing or eating, her full mouth wide open as she savored whatever was before her.

The cellist had played the last long note, and a man approached the podium, no one Morna recognized; he was dark-haired and suited, someone long accustomed to being a full-grown man.

Morna was giving her entire strength to holding Thomas upright. She looked for a chair she might guide him to, but saw nothing nearby. Sound gusted through the church as the so-called celebrants reassembled themselves, whispering, changing positions, readying for what was next. No one seemed to see Morna's predicament.

"I can't do this," Thomas said, directing his soggy words straight into Morna's ear.

"I'm Philip, Isabel's oldest brother," the man said. "I know you're all here because you loved Isabel as much as we did."

"Were you sitting somewhere?" Morna whispered.

"Up front." Thomas's addled blue irises were inscrutable.

The most efficient way to get up front was down the center aisle. She off-loaded her trench coat and heaped it on top of his, secured her grip around his waist, and the two shuffled forward, Thomas's head dipped, angled slightly toward her. Her face was on him too, so she would not have to acknowledge the scores of inquisitive eyes they were passing, like so many neon post-its. Philip was making bloated claims about death and friendship, but Morna ignored him. Under her grip Thomas still shivered, and his wet clothing gave off a peculiar doggy odor.

The first seat in the front row on the right hand side was empty. Thomas collapsed into it gratefully, still gripping her hand, oblivious to the fact that she was stranded in the aisle, hovering blimp-like above the assembled company. Someone at the end of the aisle shifted over, and after a flurry of movement a seat opened up; she took it, willing her own disappearance. As a redhead her personality had to be constantly managed. She never knew how big or small to be, how soft or loud, if she thought too well of herself, or not nearly enough. Her hair was an unfortunate light rust-red, a shade that made it hard to find clothing, that faded in summer to a grandmotherly grayish orange, and always suggested the possibility of a histrionic character or white trash origins.

When Philip stopped talking, she dared to look up. For the first time she noticed the huge black-and-white poster of Isabel mounted at one side of the stage. In it Isabel was laughing, her lips parted, so you could see the tip of her tongue that Morna knew for a fact was large and avid. The high contrast reproduction accentuated the extremes of her face—the black

Redhead

of her eyes and her hair, the pallor of her skin, the features themselves so big Morna had never been able to decide if they were beautiful or garish.

Thomas bent over to retrieve a paper under his chair. He slipped it onto Morna's lap. A poem by Pablo Neruda: "I Remember You as You Were."

"Read it for me," he whispered. "I can't." He didn't wait for her answer; he knew she would. "He was Iz's favorite poet." She heard in his querulous whisper a need that, in their eight months together, she had never witnessed.

The hall was cadaver-quiet when she mounted to the podium, except for a slight thrumming that she understood to be rain. The lights above her were bright, theatrical, not like church. It was a dream, faces you knew and didn't know merging in front of you, saving you one moment, deriding you the next. The only face that came clear to her was Thomas's, bleached and blotchy, raised to her like a chalice.

She read slowly so as not to trip over the unfamiliar words. She could feel herself flushing. She had the telltale skin of a redhead; with the slightest wisp of emotion in the air—her own or anyone else's—blood rushed to her doomed vessels like water to a Bangladeshi flood plain. "Dry autumn leaves revolved in your soul," she concluded. Done. "Neruda was Isabel's favorite poet," she said quickly. Sniffling and rain mingled with the echo of her platform-heeled boots as she descended, step by clunking step.

She stationed herself at the food table alone, suddenly ravenous. There were chicken skewers, sushi, spanikopita, bruschetta with chevre and salmon spread, brownies and petit fours. White wine was being served, and no one seemed to be holding back, as if now were the real celebration.

She had abandoned Thomas, or had he abandoned her—like

81

the entire history of their relationship it was impossible to tell. Anointed by his tragedy, he was deluged with caretakers; everyone wanted to stand in his aura. He hung on them, drank their condolences. His color was regularizing, and his ringlets were springing back to life.

There were bowls of garlic-infused olive oil, and the warm bread was porous so the oil settled perfectly into its pockets. Eventually she would have to talk to people—she'd seen a few former acquaintances eyeing her—but for now she had tunnel vision. Olive oil, food of the gods, dripped from her lips, and she leaned forward, grabbing a napkin to protect her sweater.

"You remind me so much of her." A woman who could only be Isabel's mother stood in front of Morna, studying her with a frank gaze. She was tall as Isabel had been, with a corona of upswept hair that billowed in certain places inexplicably, not shiny like Isabel's, but still adamantly brown. She had the same full regal body that Isabel had had, though her breasts had capitulated to gravity, and maybe grief. Silver disks, costume jewelry, hung from her ears, and a matching disk lay at the base of her throat. The only nod to funeral tradition was a crocheted black shawl over her ecru rayon dress.

"I'm Esther, Isabel's mother." She reached out and took Morna's oily hand. "Your reading, you make me weep." The French accent was unmistakable. "Such a gift. Morna, that is your name? When you read I can see my Isabel standing right next to you."

Esther smiled through a fresh round of tears. "I knew it will be this way. I am a piece of seaweed." Her fingers warbled, became minnows, swam out to sea.

"Yes," Morna said.

"I piece her together. Everyone here is a little bit of her—you know, DNA. I learn many things I never know before. Daughters are secrets tight from their mothers." Esther sighed, and

Redhead

a ghastly, guttural animal sound erupted from her, followed by a pudding'ish burp. Was this a prelude to something much worse? Morna waited, terrified.

"It will get better," Morna said. "They say it gets better."

"Oh. Do you really think so? I don't believe that."

Morna hated to contradict people, and she really had no idea. Philip appeared and wanted to talk to his mother privately.

"Philip, this is Morna, friend of Isabel. Her reading is so lovely?"

"Yes, lovely." But he didn't smile, didn't even seem to see Morna despite her red hair. Esther, before being whisked away, leaned down to Morna's ear, bringing an entire world of scents, along with her nimbus of grief. "Thank you for taking care of our Thomas. I like to know you. You have some stories for me, I think."

Whitney Vandermeer accosted Morna. She and her boyfriend were both in medical school. "I work in film," Morna said, when pressed. She had no actual film job at that moment. Isabel had been dead for four weeks, the exact amount of time that Morna had been un-partnered and unemployed.

"Have we seen any of your work?" Whitney wanted to know.

Morna smiled hard. There were the YouTube pieces with the stuffed armadillo, but god, she wouldn't mention them. After a year and a half of soul-killing production assistant work, she was up for a script supervisor position on a low budget slasher film. She'd never been a script supervisor before, but she was a quick study and had cobbled together a resume that led to the conclusion of experience; not an outright lie, only a survival strategy. "I'll keep you posted," she told Whitney.

She owed Thomas a goodbye. He was still surrounded, still wallowing in embraces. She tapped his back. He spun, stared at her without comprehension, his blue eyes retracted. Behind

83

him his pack of followers seemed annoyed by the interruption. She thought he would thank her for bailing him out, but when after a moment the thanks failed to come, she was flustered.

"'Bye," she said. "Later." She fled without a hug, a touch, a further word of sympathy.

Back in her apartment she squinted in the mirror, trying to discern the structural underpinnings of her appearance. She looked nothing like Isabel. Isabel looked nothing like her. Morna's hair had no sheen; she was short and skinny; she had breasts like mosquito bites as Thomas once said. What had Esther seen?

The window remained a magnet. She sucked a cigarette and watched people leaving, lingering for wistful goodbyes at the gate under the partially clearing skies, exchanging cards and suggesting dinner plans on which they would never make good. She watched the caterers loading the empty trays into a small white van, oblivious to the famous New Yorkers buried in the churchyard beneath the cobblestones. She wondered if Isabel had been buried somewhere. If she'd stayed longer she might have found out. She thought of one of the few times, maybe the only time, she'd been face to face with Isabel. Morna was coming out of the Astor Place subway station, and Thomas and Isabel were suddenly there standing by the cube, arm in arm, idling like tourists. Thomas made the introductions: "Morna, this is my wife, Isabel." Isabel held an ice cream cone that was drooling onto her hand. "Sorry," she said, smiling but scarcely looking at Morna, intent on her cone, and accustomed to being the look-*ee*, not the look-*er*. She wore a lavender, cleavage-featuring sundress, and her hair was upswept as her mother's had been today, casual and swank. As Thomas fed Morna the pro forma status questions—work? relationships? grad school plans?—Isabel's broad raspberry tongue, busy and unabashed in its appetite, devoted itself to the cone. "Morna's dad is a neuroscientist," Thomas informed Isabel. "You know—brainy about brains." Morna smiled wanly, irked that her father was being corralled to impress this woman. What about Morna herself—had Thomas even bothered to mention to Isabel that he and Morna had once been lovers? "Beautiful hair," Isabel said as they parted.

Morna and Thomas had met when he had a show of his paintings on campus. She went because her roommate was going, and she stayed because she was riveted by Thomas. He wore a red shirt and a Jackson Pollack tie, and he guided groups of fawning admirers from painting to painting, explaining the genesis of each. They were huge canvasses, eight or ten feet tall, with bright colors overlaid with gaunt, faceless figures. Morna outstayed the other visitors. She and Thomas walked the dark paths of the campus then later drank wine in his room. "What about you?" he said. She told him about the movies she made, silly little movies that she edited on her computer, wheezy little sound tracks, noir'ish lighting, not more than three minutes long.

"Can I see them?"

"They're stupid."

"I need to see them," he said and reached out to touch her fiery hair.

His paintings confounded her. They seemed so random. How did he know what to paint? He had no clear answer. Maybe he was wired that way, he said.

Once he stretched a canvas for her, and they went to the studio together, the place where the art majors worked, off limits to others. It was a warehouse-like building with high ceilings and cement walls; overhead was a hissing, eructating duct system with white pipes wide as sewer drains. Each student was assigned to an area around the periphery or next to an island at the room's center. It was mostly deserted that Saturday morning, but for one woman named Anne who greeted them with a collegial wave and returned to her encaustic work. A few months later Morna, an anthropology major, would make a documentary film about the tribe of artists that frequented this studio.

Thomas laid Morna's blank canvas on one of his easels, adjusted his table of paints and brushes so they both had access to them, and turned his attention to a painting in progress. She looked at her blank rectangular canvas and tried to see what it told her. It was eighteen inches square, tiny compared to his. Were there shadowy people traversing its snowy surface? Were there philosophical ideas that could be embodied by choosing to make a plume of yellow or blue? Was there a girl, maybe, floating on a bed, looking blankly at the viewer out of the middle of nowhere?

The light from outside bore through the dusty windows and collided too brightly with the white of the canvas, diminishing the scanty threads of ideas she'd come with. Thomas had begun applying paint. As if in a trance he moved slowly from the paint table to his canvas, to an evaluating position several feet away, then back to his canvas with more paint. He had been known to perform this ritualistic dance for eight to ten hours at a time.

A draft barreled through, and she put on her coat. The warehouse was vast and industrial; it invited nothing, encouraged nothing. Thomas liked having a place to work where nothing intruded on his own expressive outpouring.

Morna stood over the tubes of paint—the vermillion and burnt sienna and cadmium blue. If you chose vermillion how did you ever retreat from the shapes and feelings vermillion unleashed, even when you understood it to be the wrong choice?

After an hour and a half her canvas was still blank. From a kitchenette in the corner of the studio Thomas brought coffee for her, and for Anne, and for himself. He laid the cups down wordlessly, a quick nod to Morna, then resumed his work.

Redhead

Another man and woman arrived, silencing their chat at the doorway as if entering a cathedral. They settled into their areas, locking quickly into the work at hand. Ashamed of her glaringly empty canvas, Morna turned her back to everyone, walked close to her easel, brush filled with a blob of green.

A few inches from the fibrous surface, she stared at its incorrigible white. Under such scrutiny creativity was impossible. She brought the brush to her hair and stroked. The hair stood out from her scalp so she could scarcely feel the cool paint.

Esther wanted Morna to visit. She could take the Decamp #33 bus from Port Authority, get off at Bloomfield Avenue in Glen Ridge. Esther would pick her up there. Would this Saturday work? Morna listened to the message three times. It was the Tuesday after the Saturday service. Morna had been trying not to think of the event, hadn't mentioned it to a soul, had not been in touch with Thomas, nor he with her, but there had been a flurry of group e-mails and Facebook entries about how unspeakably moving it had been.

She couldn't believe how detailed Esther's message was. A similar message from her own mother would have been vague and conditional, but Esther was not, apparently, going to take no for an answer.

After two sixteen-hour days that week on the slasher film, she'd been fired due to incomplete notes, and since then she'd been sleeping until noon, but on Saturday she was up by eight, weaving past the drunks and pushers at Port Authority by nine thirty, and sitting on a bus to New Jersey by ten fifteen. The bus galumphed through the Lincoln Tunnel, stopped once in Newark then began its labyrinthine crawl through the New Jersey suburbs.

Esther had asked her to bring a copy of the Neruda poem, and stupidly she'd agreed. She didn't have the poem, didn't have time to seek out a copy, could have e-mailed Thomas, but didn't want to get into it.

The bus let her out on a main drag that skirted the edge of a residential neighborhood. The bus driver had assured Morna that this was the right place, but she stepped out unsure, a conspicuous stranger. People made armpit jokes about New Jersey, but this wasn't half bad, a rolling park on one side of the street with enormous, newly leafed maples, on the other side commodious, well-maintained houses.

It took her a moment to realize that the maroon Cadillac on the opposite side of the street was waiting for her. The driver was waving—Henry, Mr. Barrett, Isabel's father. Morna had seen him at the funeral. He was tall and quiet and formal, a black hole of a man, neither French nor interesting, not at all like Esther. He made no attempt at small talk as they drove the short distance to the Barrett home.

"My wife is inside," Mr. Barrett said. "I'm afraid I must go to work. She'll bring you back to the bus stop herself."

He drove off, leaving Morna on the sidewalk in front of a large, two-story wood-frame house, Cape Cod blue, with a well-tended front yard and a porch. It was comfortable certainly, but conventional, and she couldn't imagine pretentious Isabel growing up here, playing soccer or kick the can with the other kids on the cul de sac.

The door opened before Morna even knocked, and Esther vacuumed her in, breathless and maternal as she kissed Morna on both cheeks and ushered her into the living room. Lace curtains dimmed the light from outside so Morna had to blink several times before the room came to life. Small wooden tables with doilies and teacups. Chests with glass doors holding vases and china. A grandfather clock. A bay window with leaded glass and a window seat. It was a room that whispered of past generations, past centuries.

Redhead

Esther sat Morna on the couch and took a seat next to her. She seized both of Morna's hands in hers. "I look forward to this all week." She sighed. "I don't do so well. And you?"

In the church Esther had looked not young exactly, but sophisticated and stylish in the way of European actresses, embracing her age like Sophia Loren. In her own home, however, she seemed quite a bit older; her skin had a waxy transparency; it flaked a little; and tick-like dollops of ivory makeup clung to her hairline. Beneath her navy skirt her thick legs were sausaged into hose that looked as if they'd been prescribed. That and her powdery lavender scent suggested that Esther was closer in age to Morna's grandmother than to her mother.

"It's hard to stop thinking about her," Morna agreed.

"Do you bring the poem?"

Morna's palms in Esther's capacious hands began to slicken. "I'm so sorry. I forgot."

The skin of Esther's face, unhinged from its underlying bone structure, slipped a little. "Oh well, not today. Another day." She withdrew her hands and shored up a sagging section of her hair, gazing at the carpet, absorbing the disappointment. When she looked back up she seemed to be pitying Morna, as if she understood Morna's pathetic life precisely.

"When you read that poem you break my heart. Then you put it together. You know Isabel. If someone is known—what more can there be?"

"I won't forget next time," Morna said, miserable in her failure, on the verge of tears and finding it unbearable that she would cry in Esther's presence for all the wrong reasons.

"I have prepare us some lunch. First—an *aperitif?* I show you photos of Isabel I think you have not seen."

Morna excused herself to the bathroom to regroup, and when she came out Esther had laid out two delicate glasses on a small doily-covered table. On her lap was an open photo album, and she leaned against the couch back, her face awash in a cascade of silent tears that brought with it snail trails of eyeliner. Morna wondered if she should offer a gesture of comfort, or if Esther preferred to ride it out alone. After a moment of internal debate she extended a tentative hand to Esther's lap, squeezed the soft navy skirt and the womanly thigh beneath.

Esther regarded Morna gratefully, almost lovingly, and Morna was relieved that, for once, she had made the right choice. With the back of her hand, Esther swabbed her tears. "With her sister—she make things *difficile*, you know."

Morna lifted her eyebrows. She had identified the sister at the funeral from a distance. She was smaller than Isabel and Esther, with more pointed features. Morna didn't even know her name, let alone how she might be making things difficult.

Esther lifted her glass. "*A ton santé.*" She drank with a considering, possibly warning eye on Morna. "I think I understand why Isabel keep you to herself."

The photo album documented the activities of a young family: birthday parties, backyard picnics, sailing in Maine, a family trip to Washington, D.C. Esther pointed to Isabel in each photograph. At nine or ten she'd been lanky and long-haired, orb-eyed, face always angled to the camera and painted with her signature, full-lipped, captivating smile.

"She is born to joy. Some people are that way—from babies." They gazed at a sequence of images that captured Isabel doing a cartwheel, wearing a white skirt and white tank top. In the final picture her arms were raised in a triumphant V, her smile goofy, the image of an endearing entrepreneurial show-off, someone who might, as an adult, be either scorned or admired.

Morna's mother did not keep photograph albums, so Morna could not say how the summer vacations of her childhood had been spent. So many days, so many hours, it was scary to tally them. Swimming at the local pool was all she could remember, coming home in the evenings dizzy and slightly nauseated after so many hours in the water, waking up in the mornings still smelling of chlorine, but was there a single picture recording those days of swimming? If so, she'd never seen it.

Esther skipped over the pictures of the other three children—the sister, Philip, and one other brother, Peter—but Morna noticed that there weren't as many photos of them. Isabel was clearly favored. Even in the group photographs she showed up most clearly, always in the center, always smiling, her fierce focus on the camera's lens burning through the fourth wall. Was Esther aware of feeding Isabel's ego, of making her feel more important than the others?

"Oh, there's Dimitri," Esther said, laughing quietly. "You remember that story? I always wonder what happen to him."

Morna had not had any breakfast, and after a few sips of the sweet white wine she was light-headed. Alcohol in the afternoon was surely stronger than at night, she thought, but Esther had almost finished her glassful, and it seemed to have energized her. She rose suddenly, as if she could un-wilt herself at will.

"*Viens. À table*! You tell Isabel stories. Bring your glass."

Sunlight streamed into the dining room, flirted with the polished silver, the water and wine glasses, the hand-painted china. "We have a bit of soup, a bit of sandwich."

Esther would not allow help, made Morna sit, pour the wine if she insisted on doing something, and soon they both sat with bowls of white bean soup, plates of ham and cheese sandwiches on crusty bread, glasses of chilled white wine, less sweet than what they'd been drinking earlier. Did they always dine this way, Morna wondered, or was her visit an occasion?

"I am alone many days. Everyone is back in their life. Henry, he lose himself in work. He take off days, but he must go back now. I am terrible company. The sadness, it comes in like the wind. But you know this." She sighed. "I talk too much. Eat. Drink. Then perhaps you talk."

Morna thought of her own days as an unemployed person, treading a rail of loneliness, her efforts to find work erratic and made more difficult by her tendency to sleep until mid-afternoon. Esther took up her spoon and slowly stirred the dollop of pesto into the sea of steaming white beans. A tear plunked into her bowl, rolling slightly before dissolving into the soup. She began to laugh. "My life, you see. Cry in the sugar bowl. Cry in the soup." She laid down her spoon and took up her glass. "*Merci*." She drank, chuckled, drank some more.

Morna was on a high wire, aware she would soon have to speak.

"You come to the church without anyone. You have a husband? A boyfriend?"

Morna stirred her soup in the same contemplative way Esther had, the pesto swirling out into patterns like tea leaves, spelling obscure meanings, possibly lies, the one true thing microscopic, and for all practical purposes, invisible.

"My boyfriend dumped me." The word dumped, spoken aloud, embodied her humiliation perfectly. Tyler, boring Tyler, had given her the boot. Tyler, who had worshipped her for over a year, begged to move in with her; now, only six months after moving down from Boston, he was gone. He said Morna was too cynical for him, and he left her in the weeds to decompose.

"Oh, no!" Esther was indignant. "This man knows nothing. That is what I tell Isabel in high school when her first boy, as you say, 'dumped' her. Does she tell you? Heartbroken." Remembering, Esther laughed, eyes floating in tidal grief. "I let her stay .home from school. We eat ice cream together. But it is good for her, it make her tough. A beautiful redhead like you who can read a poem so beautiful—this man is no good for you."

"Thank you," Morna said.

Redhead

"In the end she is lucky with Thomas. From the beginning he is so broken, but he always loves her strongly. She is fragile, but he is more fragile. He does not call. Do you think he is all right?"

Thomas, robust and beloved by all, had never been fragile. Morna couldn't stand to think of the way he'd used her in his mourning as he'd always used her. Nor could she stand to think of how he'd once sat at this table, sucking up to Esther and earning her adoration. "He'll be all right," Morna said. She wanted to steer the conversation to Esther's own life, her years in France, but any subject other than Isabel seemed disrespectful.

"I cannot stop thinking of her feet. In the end they hurt so much, you know? And there is nothing to do. Not a thing to do."

"Was I a happy child?" Morna asked her mother on the phone.

"Oh, Morna, what's the problem now?"

"No problem, I'm just curious. Was I mostly happy, or mostly unhappy?"

"You had tantrums."

Morna didn't remember tantrums.

"That black watch coat you hated when you were in second grade—remember? You cut off its collar so you wouldn't have to wear it."

Morna didn't remember. Well, she remembered the coat, not the cutting.

It rains this afternoon. I make a fire. Like winter and I am bear in a cave. I pour myself a glass of wine. I think about our lovely visit. Thank you. You come again soon.

Morna spent a long time crafting an energetic response,

creative and comforting, trying to inhabit the lovely girl that Esther saw her to be instead of the snarky one who had once, momentarily, wished Isabel out of existence.

Morna hadn't thought much about feet before Esther's gnarly left extremity lay in her lap. The toes were exceptionally long and skinny, their tips small eraser heads, the nails tough and dappled with red specks of months-old nail polish. The foot itself was lean and arched, its gently spatulate bones and tendons visible, an enormous red bunion skewing the angle of the big toe.

Morna had planned this in advance. She had brought oil and towels with her, had suggested the massage. Esther was game for anything. "You do this for Iz, no?" She had removed her prescription pantyhose right there in the living room, had adjusted the pillows on the couch, and had lain back with surprising alacrity. Whatever Morna had in mind would certainly be to her liking.

But now Morna was stymied. She had never actually done this before and hadn't entertained the delicacy of feet. With so little flesh to grab how was she to proceed? She squirted oil on her palm and lifted the foot, cupping the bulb of the heel, her other hand taking the weight of the spotted calf. She worked the crusty heel, the bony ankle, advancing slowly toward the high arch. The oil was scented with lavender—which she thought was Esther's favorite—and it mingled with the musty, footy smell, noticeable, but not disgusting. Esther moaned with pleasure, so Morna felt encouraged and applied more oil and used her knuckle to rake the entire length of the sole. The regular rocking and kneading brought on speech.

When they were both unemployed they frequented the cheap afternoon movies, favoring old French movies with Jean-Paul Belmondo, Anouk Aimée, Simone Signoret, actors who understood how

Redhead

to penetrate the hidden surfaces of things. She and Isabel would duck from the day's accusing work-a-day brightness into the dim lobbies; the velveteen seats; the dreamy worlds of hope and wish fulfillment; the fantasia of beautiful bodies, witty words, harrowing love affairs.

They emerged at dusk, blinking and sighing, knowing how reprehensibly lazy they were, but weren't they finally happier than most, sucking the marrow of life as they did?

Esther, grief-worn, wine-filled, had drifted off. "Iz?" she said suddenly, opening her eyes, seeing her oiled feet, then noticing Morna and gradually remembering.

Morna returned to Port Authority at dusk. Altered by the wine, slowed by the massaging rhythms still in her fingers, she decided to walk downtown. The city gleamed. She veered to the Hudson where the leaden water glowed a pearlescent pink from the sun's final rays. A few people walked toward her on tender, overworked feet and, though it might have been too dark to see, she smiled. Hadn't she strolled here with Isabel, sharing a bag of Licorice All Sorts, discussing the children's book they would write?

When she had left that day Esther gripped her tightly. They were both tipsy. "You have your way with me," Esther said. "You are a bit of a devil, I see."

Behind the wheel of Esther's cream-colored Cadillac Morna had to pay extreme attention. She had never driven such a huge car, hadn't driven at all since moving to the city. Beside her Esther was quiet. She wore no makeup today, and she'd pulled her hair into a seedy ponytail. Her outfit seemed to belong to some other kind of woman—black athletic pants with a matching jacket all fashioned from some shiny fabric that chattered with her movements. She told Morna she'd had a few days that week when she couldn't get out of bed, couldn't find a reason for doing anything. She was glad Morna had come. They would be meeting Isabel's sister Adrienne at the cemetery where Isabel's ashes were buried.

The New Jersey towns they drove through were all deserted. It was the kind of summer day for a beach trip, a day of languor accompanied by tuna fish sandwiches, deviled eggs, popsicles. Esther's quiet was frightening, and Morna's ineptitude billowed beyond the length and breadth of the outsized Cadillac. Until now she had only seen in Esther the funeral's giddy aftermath and now some truer, more intransigent state of mourning had set in.

"When we couldn't sleep we would go to the cemetery," Morna said. "We'd walk and talk and sing. 'Good Night, Irene'—do you know that song?" Morna sang a few bars. "Sometimes, if it was warm enough, we'd take off our clothes, just to see if we could get away with it." Isabel thought she heard something and darted for the safety of a thick-trunked maple, forgetting her clothes. What a sight she was, surprisingly nimble, bare ass swaying and glinting, only emerging from the tree when Morna began laughing.

Esther touched Morna's forearm.

A web of narrow roads afforded access to all the cemetery plots. Morna drove at five miles an hour past stately, broad-leafed trees. Esther leaned forward, peering through the windshield, instructing Morna to turn, turn, turn again. They went up hills and down, circled, found themselves in the same place they'd begun.

"*Mon dieu.* I am lost. I am so sorry."

Morna turned off the engine, and they were both stricken with a harrowing case of inertia. Esther withered against her seat back. It was wrong for Morna to have come here with so many spirits at large.

Redhead

Adrienne drove up in a red Ford Fiesta and they followed her.

"I should stay in the car," Morna said when Adrienne had parked and was leaping from her car, frowning. Unlike the other Barrett women she had short hair, and a lean body that, in its tight-fitting jeans and black T-shirt, suggested a spear.

"Oh, no." Esther looked stricken. "Please. I am so afraid."

The heat was shocking again after the air-conditioned car. Adrienne had taken off through the grass, winding around trees and headstones; Esther hooked Morna's arm and they followed, Esther's suit rustling irreverently.

Isabel's headstone was a rectangle of white granite, substantial but simple. Wilted white roses lay at its base. *Isabel Picard Barrett. Adorée.*

"Ta-da. The angel," Adrienne said.

"You remember Isabel's friend Morna?"

Adrienne blinked. "Thomas's friend."

"She and Isabel do naughty things together. *Très méchantes.*" Esther chuckled and patted Morna's forearm, her arm still linked in Morna's.

"Really?" Adrienne's gaze was trenchant as the rest of her body. "I never heard her mention you."

"Some things we keep to ourself—we must have secrets," Esther said. "They write books together. At night they dance naked."

"Woop de doo."

Seeing Adrienne's niggardly smile, Morna's heart raced. "Aren't you sad?" she said.

"Of course I'm sad. I can do sad in Philly perfectly well on my own. Sad isn't some performance you do for an audience to get them to clap."

Morna nodded, but Adrienne's attention was on other things, far from here.

"Everyone thinks they own her. Who's got the right to the biggest load of grief."

Morna said nothing and Adrienne, playing the moment, scanned the cemetery where hazy sun and heat clung like lint.

"She and I always had issues. Just as we're maybe getting a teeny tiny grip on things, she had the audacity to die." Adrienne wiped the air. "Boring old business that only concerns me. Okay, are you satisfied, Mother? Can I go now?"

"You come back to the house? I make some *crème caramel* for you."

"I have to get back," Adrienne said. She spun. "I'll call." She retraced her steps to her car and drove off.

"You see," Esther said.

"Is she driving back to Philadelphia now?"

"It is possible."

They stared at the headstone, and Esther bent to collect the desiccated roses. The stone itself was inert and unsatisfying. Morna felt sorry for Adrienne, stuck with that anger. "She could—" Morna began.

"What?"

"Nothing."

"Please," Esther begged. Her fingers were beaded with blood, but she didn't seem to notice.

Morna hesitated. "Isabel just gave people the brush-off sometimes, as if they weren't as important as she was."

Esther blinked. She looked down at her fingers, suddenly noticing the blood.

Morna sat at Veselka alone in front of a pile of soy-sauce-soaked noodles for which she had no appetite. She'd brought a book of Neruda poems, but she couldn't get into them. Some man who was sick of being a man, another who was looking at blood, daggers and women's stockings—who the fuck cared.

Redhead

Since the firing she'd felt tainted. Her friend Gina, who was a film student and terminally busy, had canceled tonight at the last minute, verifying somehow that Morna was a loser. Around her students bent toward one another, talking endlessly, endlessly animated. Many of them were film students, talent-less but still thick with prospects. She hated their easy access to parental funds—the huge tuition and beyond that money to make their navel-gazing films. Isabel's family had money too, she thought. Their house was nice, and her father had one of those money-moving jobs. Maybe it was the money that made her sometimes unwittingly cruel though she'd never been cruel to Morna.

Thomas was the one who'd been cruel. She remembered too acutely the time when things began to go wrong. After months of communicating daily by phone calls and e-mail, spending at least every other night together, Thomas was suddenly incommunicado. All her e-mails and phone calls went unanswered. Three days passed, then five. She was furious. She learned that Thomas had spent several nights in his studio, crashing on a mattress he'd dragged there. Just because he was lost in his work didn't mean he couldn't pick up the phone once or twice and call her. After a week she stopped leaving messages. It was spring break. She went home to her parents' house and tried to forget him. Back on campus a week later she torpedoed the final text, crafting neutral words about needing to move on, though in her heart it was pure *fuck you*.

No one cared about you and then, on a dime, everyone appeared to. Her mother wanted her to visit Northampton that weekend for a celebration of her brother's birthday; Tyler was having a housewarming with his new partner Anthony; Whitney Vandermeer, who she'd talked to only briefly at the funeral, wanted her for dinner.

Esther prevailed. Morna brought with her a bagful of things: two bottles of Esther's favorite white wine, a sourdough baguette, a round of brie, some silver tapers, and a fat lavender-scented candle for the bedroom or bathroom, all items she was fairly certain Esther would like. She had stretched her budget, but she'd done the reckoning and wanted to feel indispensable.

Esther's delight was clear but muted. She peered into the bag and took out the bread and one of the wine bottles then left the bag on the counter like some passed-by hitchhiker. They settled at the table right away, foregoing time in the living room, so Morna wondered if Esther wanted her to leave.

"Of course not," Esther said. "I make your favorites."

She brought out dish after dish and laid them on the table: a tureen of onion soup, two roast chickens, roasted potatoes, green beans and carrots, a salad. For dessert she'd made *un gâteau framboise* that she put on the sideboard along with a cheese plate. It was enough food for an entire neighborhood, far more than she'd served Morna before. The sight of so much food sickened Morna a bit. She had gotten used to eating two small meals a day, usually composed of one dish only: eggs, a plate of noodles, a bowl of soup.

"It soothe me to cook," Esther said, but she didn't seem very soothed; she seemed to be sinking far away into a world Morna couldn't begin to reach.

"It's wonderful," Morna said, setting aside her distaste—these were her favorite dishes apparently, or Isabel's—tucking into the chicken and the crispy potatoes, using knife and fork European-style, trying to bolster Esther's mood with her own display of gusto.

"Really?" Esther said, watching Morna eat, but not picking up her own knife and fork. She sighed. "It is too much. What am I thinking?"

Redhead

"You'll have plenty of leftovers."

Morna cut and ate and drank, cut and ate more, cooing and chuckling and praising each dish as she went, trying to get Esther to follow suit, but Esther, immune, sat at the head of the table, fondling her silverware and pondering the windows, the cake on the sideboard, Morna herself. Where was Henry? Why was he never around?

Morna gulped her wine. "I don't think I've told you about the film I was writing for Isabel. She had so much potential as an actress."

"You think so?"

"She was so pretty—no, not pretty, *beautiful*. And she had screen presence."

"You see her in film?"

"We did a screen test, and her large features were so expressive. She was an amazing actress."

Esther leaned forward, hungry for this knowledge, and Morna could feel the words making pictures in Esther's mind, images she would fold into her Isabel narrative, the movie in her mind where all her daughter's dormant, unsung potential came into full bloom.

"Oh my. It does not surprise me. What is the film about?"

Morna swallowed an unmasticated piece of chicken and began to choke. Her eyes teared. Esther offered her a water glass. "Drink. Drink."

Morna drank the water and the chicken piece moved along the appropriate pathway, but Morna was left feeling sheepish and could feel the color shooting from her stressed vessels to her gullible epidermis. Esther rose and went to the front door where apparently someone was knocking. Morna tried to compose herself.

"I thought you can't come," Esther said.

"I changed my mind." Thomas.

"Wonderful. Come in. I have plenty of food and Morna tells about the film she and Isabel make."

Thomas's arrival energized Esther, and she bustled back and forth locating a plate, glasses, a napkin. Morna, still flushed and flushing anew, turned to greet Thomas, half rising from her seat, then sitting again, then pushing back her chair and standing. She couldn't hug him, not now, and he wasn't hugging her.

"Hey," she said. "I didn't expect you."

"I didn't expect myself—or you."

Morna nodded, and Thomas sat in the designated place opposite her. Morna felt disgustingly full. It bothered her that the scrim over Esther's mood had been lifted by Thomas's arrival. He had cut his hair so it bushed out around his ears. It wasn't becoming at all and he was still painfully scrawny. Esther laid a full plate in front of him. "We fatten you up," she said, laughing. She urged more food on Morna, but Morna stood her ground. The vapor of profound exhaustion had descended, and all she wanted to do was sleep.

Esther resumed her seat, but she'd forgotten the silverware. She started to get up but Thomas stopped her with a tamping palm, turned and reached into the sideboard's second drawer, helping himself to knife and fork. He ate European-style, looking around the room as he chewed as if to note its changes. After watching him for a moment Esther took up her own fork and knife.

"So," she said. "The film. You know this film, Thomas?"

Thomas's face was framed by the two white tapers. "A film. Really?" he said.

"It's not—" Morna hedged.

"We're interested," Thomas said. He laid his utensils on the side of his plate and picked up his wine glass, his gaze stitched to Morna.

Redhead

"She says Isabel has—what is the phrase?"

"Screen presence."

"And—?" Thomas prompted.

"The kind of face that reads well on film."

"Big lips, big eyes, big laugh—that kind of thing?" he said. "Big ass too—would that be photogenic?"

Morna looked down at her plate, a terrible moment returning to her in painful clarity. She and Thomas coming out of his studio. Isabel, who neither of them knew at the time, was outside talking with another woman, laughing. *What a beautiful woman*, Thomas remarked. *She's too fat for you*, Morna said. *And I happen to hate her.*

"Morna begins to tell me what the film is about."

"It's not finished, the script I mean." Morna stabbed a piece of chicken. "I was working it out."

"But the gist?" Thomas prodded.

"A girl who's—looking for—there's a maze in it like the Minotaur's labyrinth. It's based on the Neruda poem about the man walking around, sick of being a man, but in this case it's a girl." She sighed. "It's hard to explain."

"I'm sure it is," Thomas said.

"It's not realistic."

"I guess not."

"Don't be mean," Morna said, forgetting Esther for a moment, the taper flame flickering at the corner of her vision, her voice a quiet hiss, trying to lasso the part of Thomas that had once been devoted to her.

"Is that what I'm being?"

"Dessert? I get plates." Esther rose, knocking the table so the stemware rattled. She went to the kitchen and closed the swinging door behind her.

"Don't say anything," Morna whispered. "Please."

He gave her the challenging gaze she remembered him giving his canvasses: *I know you're in there. Give it up.* "Don't fuck with her. She's precious. Don't bail when it gets inconvenient, or when it interferes with your personal development."

"I'm not mean like that. She's precious to me too."

"Right. You're not the type to dispose of people."

Esther returned to the room with a tray of cake plates and demitasse cups. She maintained her silence while laying down the tray, replenishing the wine glasses with a careless flourish that made Thomas's glass overflow.

"Cake here, or in the living room? *Gâteau framboise.* Isabel's favorite." She nodded to Morna.

"I need some air," Morna said, rising unsteadily.

Outside she propelled herself through the quiet neighborhood, houses with blinds pulled, air conditioners purring, the homes of residents who kept their houses painted, their gutters clean, residents who were not cynics or practitioners of sarcasm, people who assumed the best about others. When she and Isabel were last here they had walked this neighborhood with a can of spray paint. *Breathe,* they scrawled on one stop sign. *Laugh,* one another. *Dance.*

She walked for two hours, emptying herself first of expectation, then of dread, so when she reappeared at the house she was blank and mute. Esther opened the door, as usual, before she knocked. "Thomas is gone. He has fatigue."

She had rebuilt the tower of her hairdo, retouched her makeup; her manner was assertive. She cut Morna a piece of cake and made her sit in the living room. "You stay the night," she said. "Henry is away. I don't like nights alone." She sat in the easy chair with her glass of wine and watched Morna eat. Morna was afraid to say a word, afraid of the momentum of even one syllable. She knew the cake was delicious, but her taste buds were dormant.

Esther put her in Isabel's room which was still intact, as if

Redhead

Isabel still lived there, had never left for college, never married, certainly not died. Posters of Marilyn Monroe and Audrey Hepburn. Books of poetry. Purple sheets. A red quilt. It was the room of a person with an appetite for life.

Esther had given Morna a large white nightgown, eerily bridal, once Isabel's. It was much too big for Morna, but she wore it anyway, as some kind of penance. It was only eight p.m., still light, and Morna had no idea how to fill the hours until dawn. In the morning there was an eight thirty bus back to the city; she could walk to the stop if necessary. She sat in bed listening to Esther puttering in her room at the end of the hall.

Sleepless, she ventured downstairs at two forty-five, tripping on the long white gown. She would begin with the first photo album, page through all nine of them, memorize the way families were supposed to behave. She would be able to tell if Adrienne was congenitally angry. If Isabel had always been joyful. What was truly god-given and forever in your DNA.

Esther reclined on the living room couch in the semi-darkness. She wore a lavender robe over her long pink nightgown, and she clutched a half-full wine glass. Morna thought of retreating, but it was too late, Esther had certainly heard her.

"Help yourself." Esther's voice rose like grit-filled smoke from the depths of the shadows.

Morna poured herself a fortifying glassful and sat in the easy chair, and they sipped in tense silence, Thomas a phantom between them. After a while Esther rose and disappeared and came back to the living room with her purse, still in nightgown and robe, rattling the car keys in front of Morna. "Drive me to the cemetery, *s'il te plaît.*"

It was three fifteen, night and morning both. The streets were deserted, the streetlights casting their lurid light. Morna hiked up her nightgown to negotiate the Cadillac's pedals, feeling like a criminal. She had never driven in bare feet. The iron gate to the cemetery was locked.

"Now what?" Morna said.

Esther got out and began walking. She wedged her body through a narrow space to one side of the gate and continued without looking back, eschewing the roadway. Was she crazy? Furious? Morna killed the engine and hurried after Esther's vanishing silhouette.

The grass was dewy, and Morna had to jog to catch up with Esther. She scurried along the shadow-dappled landscape, veering around monuments and headstones, slowed by the gown, twigs and pebbles stabbing her soles. This time Esther's sense of direction was infallible. Up a short rise, down, a left, another left, and they were there.

Morna stopped ten feet or so behind Esther. After a few minutes of stillness, Esther turned, "You are the expert," and she lifted the nightgown over her shoulders, and it billowed with a slight breeze. She dropped it into the grass and stood in the buff, her pale, quasi-lit body both statuesque and sagging. The matronly swoop of hip and belly, the thickly muscled calves and dainty ankles, the breasts loose as testicles. Fleshy and thin, beautiful and despairing. She waited, weight swung into one hip like Venus de Milo, hair adrift.

"*Viens*. Show me. Teach me this. We do it together."

Morna lifted her own nightgown, Esther, a cool assessing mirror reflecting back Morna's cape of redhead's freckles, her mosquito-bite breasts, the scurrilous shape of her shame. She moved closer to Esther and sat in the grass. Esther towered above her, huge and hesitant, calculating how she would lower her own frame. Morna held out her hands. Esther took one of them and, leaning against Morna's slight shoulder, lowered herself, huffing, first to her knees then rolling onto her buttocks.

Redhead

They lay down at the same moment. Side by side, they looked up through the branches of the magnolia at the faintly brightening sky. Light years away stars winked and died and continued to churn out their light.

HER BOYS

Talmadge keeps her eyes on the road while watching tiny snowflakes emerge from the pallid sky, trying to situate herself in the moment as a path to forgetting. Now what needs to be forgotten is the entire weekend trip to New Hampshire to visit her mother, Lila, and her much-younger brother, Tim. She doesn't know why she continues to make these visits, bundling her optimism into the car and transporting it up from Massachusetts where it vaporizes immediately upon her arrival.

The thing that bothered Talmadge the most on this visit was the smell of the place. It was as if a bunch of Tim's friends had been sitting around for days burping beer and pizza, farting, never cracking a door or window. They kept the heat too high—Lila claimed she couldn't adjust it—cooking the air's smell into something unbreathable. Lila, sixty-three, and Tim, twenty-four, are living together in the same house Tim and Talmadge grew up in, but it no longer resembles the tidy cozy home of her childhood. The roof leaks and some of the beige siding has come off in front and the small side yard has become a cemetery for a collection of Tim's dead vehicles. Inside there are *things everywhere,* unnecessary objects in places they have no business being. Why, for example, is there an axe in the foyer? Who has left a waffle iron on the coffee table? Why can't Tim trash his empty beer cans and rein in his cast-off sweatshirts? Throughout Talmadge's childhood the place was neat and clean, mostly due to Lila's efforts. But now even Lila leaves her own trail of sludge. She's been unemployed for the last two years, and in that time she's collected unemployment and grown fat. She and Tim have vats of excuses for their sorry state, the difficulty of finding jobs, blah, blah, blah, but Talmadge blames only their overall laziness. It's unlikely to change. And yet, once every six weeks or so she convinces herself otherwise, and bolsters her hope again and makes the visit with another envelope containing a check that her mother squints at as if it's not nearly enough.

It's Sunday afternoon and while Sunday afternoons are usually the most dismal hours of the week Talmadge now relishes the thought of getting back to work tomorrow, her boys greeting her with their usual verve and jokey sarcasm then scampering off to do what she tells them. She crosses the border into Massachusetts and her entire body goes rubbery with relief, as if the line of demarcation is as significant as an international boundary. The ebbing snow makes driving easier, but still it's not until she's back in her Somerville apartment doing the dishes, adjusting the disturbed items on her shelves (she suspects the landlord may have paid a visit while she was gone), fluffing the pillows on her bed, that she finally banishes thoughts of her embarrassing family.

Before she enters the office each morning she straightens up, brightens her face, then strides in. *It's Wendy,* she wants to call out—though she doesn't as it might offend. They aren't lost boys, but they aren't exactly *found* either. They're in their mid to late twenties and they work here at *Vitruvian*—a magazine that explores the liminal space between science and art—for a couple of years before moving on to bigger and better things. When they leave they mostly stay in touch, and she's pretty sure they look back on their employment here with some nostalgia. She strolls past their cubicles sprinkling good mornings to the early birds, grabbing a piece of Dan's bear claw as she passes for a teasing reminder of who's boss.

She loves her boys. They make her feel like a queen, not only by doing what she tells them, but by noticing her and complimenting her on her taste in clothing and shoes. Sometimes she finds herself buying something she thinks they'll like. Recently she's been eyeing a cropped red leather jacket in one of Harvard Square's high-end boutiques. She tried it on once and it fit perfectly. Its leather on her neck and bare forearms felt like the touch of a person. Now, each time she passes the window the jacket seems to nod at her, acknowledging a relationship. Someday, when the moment is right, she'll splurge. Meanwhile, even now, out of reach in the store window, it gives her pleasure.

Dave, the receptionist, beeps before she has turned on her computer or poured herself coffee. Adrian is here. She forgot—today is his first day. If she'd remembered she would have come in earlier. She and Steve, the magazine's founder and publisher, hired Adrian after a Skype interview. They gave him a month to move from Chicago.

She finds him by the front desk with Dave filling out paperwork. He stands to shake her hand. OMG, how little Skype did him justice. He is tall and loose-bodied, devoid of the usual tension of the newly hired. His thick dark brows converge in a ledge, making a secret cave of his face. The English accent, *that* she remembers, as it may have figured in his hiring. She and Steve speculated after the interview about whether his accent made him appear smarter than the American applicants,

Her Boys

giving him an edge. He was coming from a job in a biology lab that had bored him, and he was reevaluating his future, and even if the accent was misleading, with his dual biology and creative writing majors, he was just what they wanted.

She is tall, taller than most of her boys—a height that has been a useful tool in the work world compensating for whatever she lacks in the beauty department—but Adrian is taller, and from his perch he looks at her with an oblique, evaluative gaze. She wasn't prepared to be smitten. He is only thirty to her forty—older than the others, but still young. She has instituted a strict policy of not dating her boys. Once she made that mistake. Grant was his name, and after a month of rousing playful sex she realized how irredeemably puppyish he was, and she had to withdraw, and it took a couple of months of fortitude on both their parts for the mistake to mend itself, though she can still recall the humiliation. It was good, however, for reminding her: Never again.

She smiles for a fraction of a second longer than might be appropriate, offers Adrian coffee then sees he already has it. As she flushes she goes into command mode. "Follow me." For a moment it seems that her invitation might be to anywhere, to Paris, or Tibet, or to a bedroom sequestered at the back of the office.

"Steve isn't here yet," she explains. "We can never predict when he'll be in." She never shares with the new hires the precarious-sounding fact that Steve founded the magazine with the scads of money he made in hedge funds, and still keeps it afloat primarily on his own dime. "He's our guiding brain and a very hard worker, but he follows his own schedule and leaves the daily operations to me." Code for: He has his hand in so many projects *Vitruvian* is a low priority. He has a physician wife and two grown kids, one a multi-media artist, the other a molecular biologist. She's met the wife and kids a few times

111

over the years, and they know who she is, but each time she has felt how much she occupies only the margins of Steve's life. *You're the one who . . .* the wife said to her, and in that phrase it became clear she is only one of the many who manage Steve's multiple projects, the business and philanthropic involvements she knows nothing about. If *Vitruvian* folded Steve would be sorry, but it wouldn't break his heart.

Adrian walks beside her through the narrow corridors between the cubicles, their hips at almost the same level, the fabric of his navy suit jacket sending out a whir of encoded thoughts. Soon enough he'll realize a suit is unnecessary—jeans, T-shirts, and hoodies are the norm here at *Vitruvian,* though not for her. She introduces him to the rest of the boys, along with their office nicknames. Zeke the Geek. Josh by Gosh. Dandy Randy. And Dan, reliable Dan, Dan the Man who has been here the longest, almost a full four years, so she treats him as her deputy.

Adrian greets them with a nod, a smile, a laconic "Hey." She wonders what they'll end up calling him—the name Adrian is a little retentive. The suit makes him seem older than the others. Dan's bald head—which should make him look older, but doesn't—seems particularly shiny today.

"What have you done to your scalp?" she asks.

Dan fondles his pate. "Who's asking?" He winks.

"Aunt Sophie," she says.

Adrian's cool gaze shifts from her to Dan, back to her.

"You have to get used to us. We're terminally silly." She flushes, hotter this time, no doubt redder. But hell, if you can't have fun at work, what a waste. A phone call comes in, rescuing her just as she's about to feel like a serious fool.

"Dan, want to finish the tour and take him to his cubicle?"

She escapes to her office. Fuck, it's Lila. She's told Lila a million times not to call her during work hours. Tim's in trouble.

Her Boys

The neighbors, the Levys, say he stole things from their garage. Tim denies it.

"What things?" Talmadge presses.

"Well," says Lila, "a motorcycle most importantly."

Christ, why the neighbors? Stealing from some faceless corporation like Walmart she might almost understand, but the *Levys*?! Did he think they wouldn't find out? Did he think they wouldn't press charges? Mr. Levy has eyed Tim suspiciously for years, even when he was an impishly happy-go-lucky four-year-old. Everyone else was enchanted by Tim's smile back then, but apparently Mr. Levy was onto something. The smile that at four seemed to promise a charmed life, at twenty-four seems a promise of just the opposite.

"Well, what am I supposed to do? I'm not coming up there again now. I'm much too busy at work," she tells Lila. Adrian is standing outside her door, staring at her through the wedge of glass. She can't let herself get worked up. She raises a finger to him and stares down at her desk. "Okay, okay, I'll talk to him later. . . . No, not *now*, later."

But Tim is already on the line. "The garage was open."

"You think that makes it okay?"

"I'm just saying."

"Well, it's a stupid thing to say. You have to talk to them. Apologize. Give back whatever you took. Nip this thing in the bud before you find yourself in big trouble."

"I can't do that."

"Of course you can. Swallow your pride and just do it."

"Mr. Levy called me a cunt. I told him I wasn't planning on keeping it. I was only borrowing. You know."

"I don't know. Look, do whatever you want. I have to get back to work." She shuts off her phone and stares into her Escher screen saver. Tim is writing the handbook on self-sabotage. She descends some steps in her Escher universe and finds herself on a ledge above an unseen abyss. It's not the end of this Tim mess. She lays her hands on the keyboard then looks up, remembering Adrian, but he's already gone.

Dan's knock surprises her. "We're taking the new guy out to lunch. Want to join us?"

She always joins them if she's free. She sits among her boys, basking in her small lagoon of power, joining in their banter, sometimes pretending to be one of them, other times acting as their den mother, chiding them about staying up too late or drinking too much, advising them about their girlfriends. She's found ways to be part of their gang while still being able to pull rank.

"Who's coming?"

"Everyone. Omnivore at 1:00."

She salutes. Good on Dan for organizing this. She counts on him to keep the esprit strong, and she and he collaborate to keep *Vitruvian's* rituals alive. They make people run the spanking gauntlet on birthdays, dress up for Halloween, choose Secret Santas at Christmas. They howl to the full moon in winter when it's visible from one of the office windows. It's corny stuff, sure, but when everyone participates it's spirited and team-building. Playful. It embodies DaVinci's spirit. She couldn't possibly do it alone, without Dan.

Omnivore is a hip burger joint two blocks from the office, just off Mass Ave. The *Vitruvian* group is known there and does its part to keep the place in business and to keep it hip. Talmadge often thinks how odd it is that she has become an element in the calculus of hip, she who has made it the business of her adult life to conceal her family's lack of education and embarrassing dearth of sophistication. She could teach a course in how to maintain such a façade if anyone would sign up.

Her Boys

They are given a rectangular table and Adrian sits on one end, gazing from person to person in wry, amused silence. Talmadge sits next to him. She would rather be sitting a distance away so she could do the watching. Shouldn't *she* be presiding at the end of the table? Ordinarily she wouldn't care, but today, with a new employee on board, the seating arrangement seems wrong.

The topic is the end of the world. All her boys are gleeful little freighters of pessimism, clear-eyed and clearheaded about the facts of the earth's decline—the killer viruses leaping from the jungle, the islands disappearing under rising sea waters, the mega cyclones, the unstoppable fires. They know and remember arcane facts and bandy them about playfully—it's still a game to them, still theoretical, with no attendant depression or urge to suicide. Perhaps she feels a little the same way—it's fun to talk eco-gloom—but the ten or fifteen years she has on them skew things a little differently, and each time there's a polar vortex she wonders if now is the time to think more strategically about her options.

Josh is talking about NOAA's destroyed data. It'll take years for all that data to be reassembled, he says, and that won't happen until the science is held in high regard again and funding resumes. "Beyond my lifetime," he says triumphantly.

She turns to Adrian. "Ever hear such a bunch of pessimists?"

He smiles—a little mocking?—and adheres to his silence. His interview was deceptive—he was perfectly talkative then. Maybe he's just shy. But how little eagerness he exudes, what scant need to impress. The other boys were terrible show-offs when they arrived, and she worked hard to ease them from nervousness. Even Dan, relaxed with her as he can be, still defers.

She falls into silence herself. The group has been made lively by the presence of someone new, even a silent someone.

115

VANISHING

Watching them makes her proud, though their qualities of intellect and humor have nothing to do with her. When her burger comes she dives into it enthusiastically, but after two bites, feeling Adrian's eyes on her, she puts it down. She is too sheepish to look at him. By the numbers she's a normal-sized woman, but she has always seen herself as large due to her barrel chest. Her face is dominated by a wide forehead and broad cheeks. Her best feature is an aquiline nose that could be seen as patrician. She is in the habit of looking in mirrors and seeing the ruinous palimpsest of her mother's square jaw, one day to be hers.

She steals a glance at him, and he looks back with that unreadable smile that looks simultaneously flirtatious and uncertain, amicable and armoring. Armor, amour, she thinks. A trickle of sweat runs between her breasts. Her skin's flashing seems confused, even as she sweats she is letting things in. Her burger languishes on its plate.

"You're the only woman at the magazine?" he says.

"Oh," she says. "Yes. Why?"

"It doesn't bother you?"

She shrugs. What's not to love.

"You're not one of those women who hates other women, are you?"

"Of course not." She wants to ask him why he asked. Does she appear to be that kind of woman? It occurs to her she doesn't know if he has a girlfriend. He hasn't mentioned a partner, and she has assumed he doesn't have one, though maybe she's wrong. None of the other boys have mates. It's not a requirement for hiring, it's simply the way they are at this age, uncommitted yet to anything, enjoying their fluidity.

She has given Adrian an article to edit. It's really a photo essay with a few accompanying statements about the demise of glaciers above the Arctic Circle. The photos of the ice are

Her Boys

stunning, sensual. Huge icebergs calved from the glaciers, tall as skyscrapers but far more shapely, in pale shades of blue and mint, floating in darker cerulean water. She has spent a great deal of time looking at these photos, wondering if beauty almost always portends something dire. On the basis of recent *Vitruvian* articles alone, one might conclude that. Another recent article featured newly discovered viruses whose beauty under the electron microscope was breathtaking, then deeply disturbing when you remembered they were agents of the worst routes to death. She oversees everything but she knows very little about the science itself. Or the art for that matter. She got the job because she met Steve when he was just starting out and looking for someone he could rely on. Reliable she certainly is. She's organized, a good synthesizer and delegator, a reasonably good communicator. Privately, she finds this convergence of art and science elusive, wonders if the juxtaposition reveals anything useful. She keeps these thoughts to herself, however, because Steve believes in the magazine's mission fervently, all the more since the advent of what they only half-jokingly call 'The New Order.'

Adrian comes to her office three times that afternoon with questions he could have emailed. Each time he wears that masking smile. "The Oxford comma," he says on the third visit.

If it's a question she can't tell. It has been forever since she's discussed the Oxford comma, and now it takes her a second to locate herself and focus on the strength of that comma.

"What are you asking?" she says.

"Do we use it?"

"Absolutely. In certain cases it's critical to clarify meaning."

"Meaning." He smiles toward the floor as if she's quaint, as if the whole idea of meaning is antiquated. As he examines the linoleum she thinks he might be right, they probably *should* question meaning, how stupid not to. He closes her office door quietly, almost covertly, and vanishes back to his cubicle. Each time he departs she finds herself inhabiting a quiet lacunae of inactivity.

At least she had the good sense not to bring Grant to her Somerville apartment. It's a dim two-bedroom, sizeable enough, but a little lackluster, notable mainly for its remarkable tidiness. She understands how constipated it looks with its many collections of tiny things: miniature boxes, ivory figurines, dozens of smooth beach pebbles half the size of a pinkie nail. Her response to small things is immediate and involuntary. They arouse the *aww* response most people reserve for babies.

She can't stand the thought of anyone else's gaze coming to rest on these things, drawing conclusions, sensing pathology where none exists. Yes, she is a big woman obsessed with tiny things, but she is not only that woman. She isn't a control freak and she's not deprived. She has been at *Vitruvian* for fourteen years because it suits her, she likes it. She has chosen this life and feels no need to change it out for another one.

Over the next week Adrian visits her office frequently, always polite, his questions always legitimate, if a bit minor. He lingers longer than is strictly necessary, but she doesn't mind. He is a comma in her day, a dash, then an ellipsis. With each visit time stretches so a patch of wintry sunshine from her office window seems to settle around them, lustrous and pulsating, a place they might exist for a while, like a vacation snatched suddenly from a pocket. In their conversational pauses the commotion from nearby Harvard Square sounds unnecessarily crass, the emanations of human beings who have never considered meaning. She turns in the direction of a distant busking saxophonist. "Relax!" she commands. Adrian smiles broadly. They discuss only work. He is now editing an article about an artist from California whose work is inspired by the shapes of leaves. In the sunlight she sweats and her face pinkens. She searches for symptoms in him.

She could be deluded. One minute she's quite sure he's smitten too; the next, his composure tells her he's only being a good employee, trying to curry favor. How did he learn to smile so ambiguously? He wanders to her bookshelves where she keeps a dish of half-inch Guatemalan worry dolls given to her by a friend. He picks one up, squints at its featureless face.

"A worry doll," she says. "From Guatemala. You're supposed to fondle it when you're worried."

"Does it work?"

"If you believe in it, maybe. Take one. Try it out."

He lays it back in the dish. When he turns to go his smile flickers, almost extinguishes, like a wind-snuffed flame. She feels silly. Did she shame him by implying he needed a worry doll? The word fondle was a bad choice. At the door he turns.

"The magazine's mission isn't really about the convergence of science and art, is it? It's about beauty. The beauty of fractals, the beauty of neurons, the beauty of clouds and leaves and the solar system."

"Maybe," she says. "You might have a point." How did he learn to converse in this destabilizing way, saying things that seem to come from left field, making it seem as if he is either not present, or more present than anyone else in the room?

Lila calls bursting with news. Talmadge puts the phone on speaker and continues making her omelet, listening without saying much in response. She used to admire her mother, want to emulate her. That was when Lila was working as a paralegal, supporting the whole family after her husband, Tim and Talmadge's father, died. Tim was only a baby then, Talmadge sixteen. But now her mother, since being laid off, sits on the exculpating throne of ageism. *No one wants to hire an old bag like me,* she says. Talmadge has watched Lila let herself go, gaining thirty pounds, becoming the old bag she speaks of. It doesn't have to be that way, Talmadge thinks; she's still a couple of years from retirement age, she could find *some* kind of work.

She takes the omelet into the living room and sits on the couch to eat, leaving the lights off. It's cold out and the radiators are groaning and hissing as if they're furious. The Levys are not going to press charges, Lila says, isn't that great. No, Tim never apologized, she has no idea why they changed their minds. And Lila spoke to the manager at the 7-11, an old friend of hers, who has hired Tim on a provisional basis.

Her mother pauses and Talmadge stares at the phone. This is her cue to play cheerleader. *Good for you! I knew you could do it!* But the Levys *should* have pressed charges. Tim deserves it. You don't just steal a motorcycle because a garage door was left open.

"Make sure he doesn't spend his whole paycheck on beer," she says.

"Cut him some slack," Lila says. "He never had a father."

Outside urban squirrels scream like rats in the trees. She thinks of her boys, working diligently away on projects that only half interest them, until something cracks and their secret dreams explode into public. Special lives await them. But how many special lives can the world really support?

Why aren't more people exhausted by the thought of family as she is. She's never been remotely tempted to give up her independence. No kids. No marriage. She's free to travel. Free to stay up all night if she chooses. Even if she *doesn't* do these things, the thought that she *could* supports giant stadiums in her mind housing the eventual, the someday, the maybe could be.

After a few weeks of work Adrian begins to wear jeans, but he retains the button-down shirts and suit jackets which set him apart from the others. He doesn't resemble a businessman, but a man who thinks for himself. *Consider this*, he seems to be saying with all his gestures. A tardigrade. A fractal. A worry doll. The pursuit of beauty. She wonders if the amount of time he devotes to thinking would make him not so good in bed. During their group lunches she tries to draw him out, talking about her love of New England and suggesting places around Boston and Cambridge he might be interested in exploring. He evinces only subdued interest at best. She asks him about what he likes most about the study of biology. "The structure of leaves," he tells her, a remark she cannot use as a conversational launch pad, mostly because of the clipped, almost curt way he said it. Eventually she is bold enough to ask about his writing, a sensitive subject for her boys, as many of them are secret writers with fragile autobiographical material at odds with their grandiose aspirations. His mouth twists into an enigmatic slash. "Not writing much," he says.

"What do you think of Adrian?" she asks Dan one evening when the others have left.

Dan pauses, frowns, slides a hand over his crown as if taming wild invisible hair. "He's okay. A little aloof."

She nods. "I'll say."

"He's perfectly good. He's just not one of the gang."

She nods again. Maybe it was a bad hire.

"Don't worry," Dan says. "It's not the end of the world." He collects his things, grinning the trademark grin he uses as a tincture to liven people's spirits. "It'll be fine." He pauses at her office door. "But it would be easier if Randy didn't have the hots for him."

"Oh?" she says. "I didn't—does he lean that way?"

"Who—Adrian or Randy?"

"I know about Randy."

Dan flaps his palm. "Who knows. That's the thing. No one knows. It's not obvious."

When Dan leaves she sits in her silent groove wondering if she has seriously misread things. Should she let Adrian go and thereby remove him from everyone's consciousness? But on what grounds when he's doing good work?

The end of the world never arrives fast enough, especially when you wait for it. Dan likes to say this. She reminds him a meteor could crash at any moment. She likes to imagine such a collision being predicted a week or two in advance—impossible, of course, but when does the imagination defer to fact. In her vision people dash around, knowing what's coming and trying to put their affairs in order, as if their affairs still mattered. She wouldn't be one of the dashers, however. She would watch the mania from a wry distance. On the appointed day she would savor the sky erupting into shades of red and orange then etiolating to extreme whiteness. As retinas were being seared and people were stumbling around in semi-blindness, she would still be watching at some remove, welcoming the end. She has a soundtrack to accompany this vision. It begins with atonal cacophony that deliquesces to a single note, a melancholy oboe that dies out slowly as blackness takes over. How comforting it is to think of a time when matters of the future, sex and work and family and meaning, will finally be immaterial.

The transition to spring is problematic. The light is inscrutable, useless for telling time. During the winter months she leaves the office in darkness; now, however, stepping into the still-sunlit streets is too much exposure. She feels the whiteness of her legs and the fleeting gazes of strangers assessing her. Her pallor. Her size. Her singleness.

Another disturbing aspect of the transition to spring is they all depart at different hours. In the depths of winter when it

Her Boys

gets dark just past 4:00, they all leave as a group reliably at 5:30. But now at 4:45 a restlessness sets in, and Randy begins to pack up. Zeke is usually next. Josh and Dan often stick around past 6:00 or 7:00 when their projects demand extra work. She stays as long as necessary to lock up—unless the last person is Dan who also has keys. She hates the feeling of her work force dribbling away.

Today, a few minutes before 5:00 Adrian and Dan parade past the cubicles to the front door, Dan's body bobbing up and down with each step, his pate unmistakable, smooth and inviting as the skin of a ripe mango. Adrian floats past without any obvious up and down motion. They're conversing with great animation, surprising for Adrian, though not for Dan.

She hurries out and finds herself in the reception area with nothing to do. Dan spins and backtracks to his cubicle to retrieve something, *hey* in passing. She stands with Adrian and receptionist Maven Dave, who has begun to pack his things.

"Cashing it in early?" she says to Adrian, hearing the words sound like a reprimand when she meant them as a joke. Adrian raises his eyebrows and looks at his watch, turning its digital black to her. 5:01, it reads. "Everything's coming along okay?" Locked in, she has no idea how to shift gears.

Dan returns, holding his phone aloft. "Don't let this woman give you guff," he tells Adrian, elbowing Talmadge playfully.

"What are you boys up to this evening?" *Home, bed,* is Dan's standard teasing reply to this question. *We young people get tired too.*

"Catching the new Jarmusch movie," Dan says.

Adrian's face absorbs her, taking thorough inventory. He and Dan seem like people she has spotted on another train traveling in the opposite direction. The Jarmusch movie. She remembers hearing a review of it, but can't remember what the review concluded.

"That should be good," she says.

"Hope so." Dan shrugs, beset with uncharacteristic impatience. "We'll tell you tomorrow."

She's a spider dangling above a possible location for a web. She could suspend herself forever deciding. She might have hung herself from the wrong place. Dan and Adrian disappear, gabbing again as soon as they pass through the door. Within twenty minutes the others have left too, except for Josh who tells her he'll be done by 6:00.

She wanders aimlessly past the cubicles. Dan's has always been cluttered with tchotchkes and slips of paper, *two-day talismans,* he once said, defending himself. Fortune cookie prophesies. A found keyring with the hologram of a stripping girl. Glow-in-the-dark stars. A blowup hippopotamus from an amusement park. Above his desk is a calendar she's never noticed. The month of March is displayed with a closeup of a strange blue insect. The fifteenth is blocked out with a black X. The Ides of March—or is there a more obscure meaning? Adrian's cubicle is spartan by contrast. He has equipped it with black accessories for pencils and pens and papers. A black stapler and black pencil sharpener. It could be a display in an office supply store, devoid of personal details. She's tempted to open the desk drawers, but she doesn't because Josh is nearby and it would be obvious she was snooping.

Steve puts in one of his surprise visits in late March. These surprise visits used to unnerve her, make her feel as if he was checking up on her but, now that she knows he trusts her, she has adjusted to his unpredictability. They often go for coffee to chat about ideas for upcoming issues, the magazine's general direction, sometimes fundraising. She enjoys Steve's peripatetic mind. He has an interest in everything and credible knowledge of so much—ornithology, medicine, music, fine art. His grasp on so many subjects puts her to shame, and, for a man who knows more than most, he's not a bad listener either. She only offers a suggestion if it's something she's considered for a while and has real merit.

Today he's his usual shabby self—baggy khakis and a worn red corduroy shirt he once told her dates back to college. His hair, rumpled as Boston lettuce and badly in need of a cut, wisps around his neck and down into his eyes. She is still, after years of knowing him, trying to detect if his dressing style is a result of his living more in his mind than in the physical world, or if it's a strategy to deflect speculation about the size of his bank account.

He announces himself at the door of her office and they exchange a few pleasantries, then he spends an hour in his office before coming back to announce he is taking Adrian to lunch. She can't tell, for a second, if he's inviting her too, and then she realizes he's not. She watches them leave the office, ambling side by side past the cubicles, Adrian lively as he was with Dan, smiling even as they exit the front door.

Steve doesn't connect with everyone but, if the cant of another mind is similar to his, he detects this immediately and something alchemical happens. Judging from what she's just seen, that alchemy is happening now.

Adrian is gone with Steve for almost two hours, and he returns to the office alone and disappears immediately into work at his cubicle. She realizes Steve must have come to the office for the sole purpose of meeting with Adrian. Of course he'd want to know his new employee, but the thought of them over lunch without her for a full two hours makes her feel as if they were discussing something covert. A coup perhaps, Adrian replacing her. Would Steve feel more comfortable with someone like Adrian—younger and male and more conversant with science—running the show?

VANISHING

She finds an excuse to visit Dave in reception and passes Adrian's cubicle. His posture is straight and still, but for his typing fingers, his face composed and serious as if what he is doing, who he is, is so much more important than everything about her. She can't bring herself to puncture his concentration.

In a strange convergence her mother and Dan share the same birthday in early April. April 8th. Lila is turning sixty-four and, as always, wants Talmadge present for a celebration. There are few occasions Talmadge dislikes more than these birthday celebrations of Lila's which are occasions for an uptick in Lila's complaining about the world and her position in it. Talmadge rarely has any credible reason for bowing out. Last year she said she was sick, but that won't fly two years in a row. The 8th falls on a Friday this year, so she agrees to go to New Hampshire for a Saturday dinner. She'll spend the night, return on Sunday. Short and sweet and still the dutiful daughter.

For Dan's birthday, his twenty-eighth, she makes plans for champagne and cake and hors d'oeuvres to be delivered to the office a little before 5:00, a surprise she has apprised everyone of, except of course, Dan himself. She always makes a big deal about birthdays, due to her general belief in ritual, but Dan deserves a little extra, given what a pillar he is. And this year he's twenty-eight on the 8th which seems notable. In the past she's taken him and one or two of the others out for drinks, but she likes the less inhibited option of having a celebration in-house. She visits a party store in Waltham where she orders a bouquet of helium balloons, and comes away with bags of streamers and plates and napkins and silly hats and the blowers common at birthday parties when she was a kid. A week or so before the occasion she notices the moon will be full on the 8th. Some howling is in order—what a bonus!

126

Her Boys

"Plans for your birthday?" she asks Dan.

"The usual."

"That being?"

"Drunkathon. Drown my sorrows. What else compensates for getting so old."

"Yeah, right." She makes a face.

"We can't all be ageless like you."

She swats his shoulder. "Upstart," she says. "Get to work. Hey, how was the Jarmusch movie?"

He blanks for a moment. It's been several weeks. "Oh. Great. Plotless as usual. Well, there is some plot, but it doesn't kick in until close to the end. You might not like it."

"I love plotless. My whole life is plotless."

He shakes his head. "Don't undersell yourself."

She never gives her boys presents, but this year a present for Dan seems to be in order. She'll have to slip it to him in private so it won't be seen as favoritism. He's a big reader—a book seems like a good choice. No, a gift certificate to the Coop so he can choose himself. On the Wednesday evening before the Friday party she hits the Coop at lunch to purchase some poster board for a Happy Birthday sign. On the ground floor before buying the gift certificate she pays her ritual visit to the science section where she browses the coffee table books. There's one she frequently returns to when she's feeling unsettled. It's called *Blue/Green/Brown Planet* and it contains dozens of photographs taken of Earth from space. The book's intention is to show the extremity of climate change already underway, but the photos are mainly compelling for their beauty. She wonders if it's wrong to admire what is devastating, but nevertheless the photos never fail to diminish her own paltry anxieties.

She looks up and there is Adrian, back to her, also immersed in a book. The reticulations of his long bare bent neck bring to mind the spikey spine of an iguana. She freezes, wanting and not wanting him to see her. If he does see her she's afraid it will appear she's stalking him. She inches quietly to the register. As she waits, he takes a place in line a few people back. Now he's the one stalking her, and it's his place to initiate conversation first. Of course he doesn't. She leaves the store with perfectly constructed tunnel vision that eliminates him.

Out on the street she hesitates, then takes a right turn away from the office. Her red jacket is still in the window, today an irresistible Siren. She goes in and removes her sweater and tries it on, bare-armed, creating a moment of privacy in the eye of the salesgirl's blather. She shivers beneath the soft stroking hide of an animal that once had a pumping heart. "Yes, it's gorgeous," she agrees with the girl, "but not quite yet."

The conference room is a windowless room adjacent to reception and, with Maven Dave's help, she is able to decorate and usher in the balloons and cake and champagne and trays of catered food without anyone else noticing. She posts the crude HAPPY BIRTHDAY poster she has made, and with the assistance of a ladder she and Dave tape streamers to the ceiling so they fill the room like beaded curtains. Normally she would do this kind of thing with Dan, laughing and chatting and acknowledging how juvenile they were being. Dave is a good worker, but he's quiet and too submissive to be a barrel of fun.

Everyone but Dan has been instructed to come to the conference room at 4:50. Presumably Dan, finally alone, will come to investigate and they will yell *SURPRISE* and begin popping champagne corks. Dave locks the front door at 4:45, and she and he go to the conference room. The room looks pretty darn good, the balloons floating among the labyrinth of dangling streamers. The catering is top drawer: several kinds of

Her Boys

bruschetta, olives, crudites, gourmet crackers and cheeses. The poppyseed cake says: DAN THE MAN. No Happy Birthday. No number. Only DAN THE MAN.

The others file in, one by one, Zeke, Josh, Randy, and finally Adrian, their expressions furtive more than mischievous. They whisper. Within a minute or so Dan is in the doorway, grinning. "Surprise!" she says loudly, and the others echo her, speaking rather than shouting, more subdued than she hoped.

Dan nods, still grinning, though obviously not shocked. "Thanks guys. Just what every twenty-eight-year-old needs."

"You knew?" she says, a little crestfallen.

"I know *you*. I thought you might do something, but I didn't realize it would be so elaborate. Twenty-eight isn't exactly a milestone."

"Dig in," she says. "Drink up."

Champagne is poured. People help themselves to small plates of food and stand around filling their faces, batting balloons and streamers away from their plates, saying little. *Talk*, she wants to say, *laugh*! Adrian has taken neither food nor champagne. He has caught one of the balloons and he palms it near his waist, eyeing the ceiling and the sloppy taping of the streamers. Randy has sidled over to him. She looks for secret signals between them, but sees none.

She stands with Dan and gulps her champagne. They're all acting like kids finding themselves at an adult occasion they can't wait to escape. It was never like this before. She's misjudged something. Dan goes through his champagne as fast as she does. "I gotta pace myself," he says as she pours them more.

"Plans later?"

He shrugs.

"It's a full moon. You know what that means."

He smiles. She's never seen him so stiff. What's his problem?

"We need music," she says. "Hey, Dave, can you get some

music in here?" An oversight to have forgotten music—it's as good a social lubricant as alcohol, sometimes better, and Dan loves to dance.

Dave sets up his phone with a small blue tooth speaker and streams a rapper. Not what she had in mind, but it'll have to do. Zeke and Josh are mouthing the words: *Bad thang, fine as hell, thick as fuck. . . .*

"Good looking cake," Dan observes. "You thought of everything."

"Music. I forgot music."

"You got it now."

"Yes, I do. The hostess with the most-est. Hey, what's up? Why are you being like this? Someone told you about the party, didn't they?"

Dan reaches for the cheese plate and palms three cubes which he tosses into his open mouth basketball-style. He speaks through the cheese. "Yeah. Hey, thanks for the gift certificate. You didn't have to. Really."

"I know what I have to do. You don't need to tell me. Stop being so damn formal." She's never chided him, not sharply like that. The others have overheard, but she doesn't care.

His eyes pop wide. He upends his champagne and lays down cup and plate. "I'm leaving. I'm going to grad school."

The champagne bubbles through her nose. She grabs a napkin and dabs her face. "What kind of grad school?"

"Writing. MFA. Fiction."

"You never mentioned—"

"I didn't think I'd get in. But I did. Arizona. Wait-listed at Virginia."

"Well, congratulations. Hey, everyone, a toast to Dan." She raises her empty cup. "He got into grad school and it's his twenty-eighth birthday. What more could a guy want, right? To soon-to-be-famous-writer Dan!"

Her Boys

"Dan," they all echo, raising their cups. But for the rap the room falls silent.

"You all knew?"

They shrug.

"Will you still need me, will you still feed me, when I'm sixty-four. . . ." The line is stuck in her brain as she drives north because Lila has been singing it to her on the phone for the last couple of weeks. Talmadge never liked that song in the first place.

The drive to Tim and Lila's takes only an hour and a half, but it is mid-afternoon by the time Talmadge arrives because she dragged her feet, stayed in bed forever, drank coffee forever, took forever to throw a few things in an overnight bag. She considered canceling on the grounds of joylessness, but Lila would never understand.

By the time it was dark last night and the moon began to show, she was the only one in the office. They'd all left as a group after forty-five minutes. Dan volunteered to help clean up, but she forbade him and he didn't protest. It was clear he had plans to continue his celebration elsewhere. Whether the others went with him, she has no idea. She ferried all the leftover food and cake to the dumpster in the alley. She popped all the balloons, the helium in them still strong enough for a good Donald Duck session. She yanked down the streamers leaving bits of paper and tape still freckling the ceiling. The remaining two champagne bottles she put in Dan's cubicle. She couldn't stand going home, so she sat in her office with the lights off waiting for the moon to appear, blaming Adrian, who she knew was blameless. The moon finally appeared in her window, taking center stage, tumescent and white. A sound emerged from her larynx that was too meek to be called a howl.

VANISHING

This day, Saturday, is punishingly beautiful, a perfect spring day, aggressively sunny, warmer than it has been of late, and animated with everyone's bustling intentions. Her only intention is to endure this next so-called celebration.

Lila prances from the house before Talmadge has even turned off the engine. She is all decked out in party clothes: a hot pink dress from which cleavage drools, a wide gold cummerbund cinched over her plump mid-line. Beneath the dress's mid-thigh hem the crepey flesh of her legs flutters with each stride. Her hair has been recently dyed brown with swaths of yellow-gold, then curled and teased over her forehead in the shape of a wary cobra, a style Talmadge has never seen before—the vogue in New Hampshire? Fringed gold earrings chitter and sway in the space between lobes and shoulders. The whole getup seems more extravagant than necessary for a family party.

"Not bad for a 64-year-old broad, right?" she says before Talmadge has a chance to weigh in.

"Stunning," Talmadge says, a kind of truth. "But aren't you dressed up kind of early?"

"It's my birthday the whole damn day. Come in. I have a surprise for you. Tim's at work. He gets off at 5:00 and we'll eat when he gets home." She waits for Talmadge to retrieve her overnight bag and the wrapped present from the trunk, a Melitta coffee maker with a thermal carafe to replace the stained, cracked Mr. Coffee she's been using for years.

"You didn't need to bring a present," Lila exclaims.

But of course she did.

The surprise is in the kitchen, a hulking male in a powder-blue polyester suit jacket and a bad black dye job. "This is Ron, but I call him Prince," Lila says, nestling her head onto his chest. "My amour. This is my daughter, Tallie."

Ron stands, winks at Talmadge and gives her a strong handshake, his eyes traveling her body unabashedly. "You don't look much like your brother."

It's true, she and Tim appear to be from different gene pools. Tim, at twenty-four, skinny and not tall for a man, is still in the process of becoming, whereas Talmadge, at forty, is substantial, a person already become. "If you're wondering if we have the same father, we do." It is unusual for Talmadge to want to claim kinship with Tim, but Ron, this prince, has that effect on her.

"Prince is in insurance," Lila says. "But I like to say he's *my insurance.*"

They exchange a look and a chuckle that forces Talmadge to look away. She excuses herself as quickly as she can to the spare room, which doubles as a laundry room, making privacy unpredictable. The dryer is running and with each rotation something metal—a zipper, a button—whaps. She supposes it's good her mother has someone, even if he's not permanent. She lies on the bed, feeling the pulse of recent humiliation and the subsequent sleeplessness, but napping here is out of the question.

Ron, to Talmadge's surprise, is making the meal, spaghetti and fried chicken. He asks Talmadge to make a salad. The two of them work side by side at the counter while Lila sits at the kitchen table with a glass of white wine, filing her nails. Ron has taken off his powder blue jacket to cook. His collared shirt, partway unbuttoned, is black, and he moves around the kitchen with an alpha swagger, knowing exactly where to locate pots and pans and seasonings.

"He's a keeper, isn't he," Lila says. "You know people think folks our age don't have needs, but we do have needs, right Prince? And we're attractive—maybe not to people of your age, but to each other, right Prince?"

"She's right." He winks, first at Lila, then at Talmadge, as if he has separate running conversations with each of them.

"Tallie doesn't tell me about her love life and I don't ask. It's not a mother's right to ask."

Tim arrives home from work after 5:00, as promised. He greets Talmadge as if he's glad she's here. She tries to be glad too. He cleans up, changes his shirt, and they sit down to eat, Ron and Lila at the head and foot of the table, Tim and Talmadge on each side across from one another as if they're still kids. Each time Ron rises to get something, he slaps Tim's shoulder or back.

Tim, who has thickened she notices, has a surprise of his own. He's just enrolled in school, two night classes at the community college. He thinks he wants to go into engineering, and the teacher of his math class says he has the chops. He beams at Talmadge just as he did as an entrancing four-year-old.

"That's great," she says. "Really great." Everywhere, the world bristles, tiny bundles of sparking intention.

The coffee maker is a bust. Ron gave Lila the very same thing just yesterday, though a higher-end model, more bells and whistles, more expensive.

"That piece of coffee-making machinery is a thing of beauty," Ron says. "Perfect coffee. So much better than that piece of shit she had. I'm sure this one is good too—keep it for yourself. I know it'll make you happy."

Tim knocks for his laundry just as she's slid into bed. "I'll be quick," he says, pulling clothes from the dryer, back to her.

"Aren't you the cozy little family," she says.

He lays his laundry basket at the foot of her mattress. "He's a good guy. And he makes Mom happy, which is something. A big thing, actually."

"I don't suppose she's still looking for a job. In case her prince doesn't work out."

"Jeez, Tallie, she's sixty-four, she's done working. It's my turn now."

"You're okay with that?"

He looks straight at her, a new habit. In the past he always looked away, even as recently as her last visit. He is no longer the devilish child embossed in her mind.

"Sure, why not."

"The Levys?"

"Forget them. We worked it out. That whole thing is history."

"If you say so. You guys need money?"

"Naw, we're good. My boss is helping me out with college and stuff. And Ron, he helps out too. Thanks though." He starts out the door, then turns. "Hey, can't you be happy for us?"

She nods. "I am."

"Good."

"Course I am," she says to his disappearing back, so quietly he might not hear.

She intended to leave early but Ron has made pancakes and bacon and eggs, and he urges her to stay, and she stays so as not to come off as a poor sport or a snob, or whatever. As a result, she doesn't make it back to Somerville until mid-afternoon. The day is soggy and chilly, a rebuke to yesterday. The familiar Sunday afternoon melancholy pervades the saturated air, dread of the next day and all its inevitable setbacks, the certainty she will have to confront her own ineptitude. She unpacks and flops around the rooms, intending to clean but not having the verve.

She perches in her kitchen's easy chair staring at the inferior coffee maker still in its box, thinking of her boys, wondering who might be a candidate to fill Dan's shoes. Adrian is

out of the question, too aloof. Dave, the receptionist, is not the brightest light. Josh and Randy and Zeke are all great guys, but they don't have Dan's backbone, and she can't see them as generators or even perpetuators of team spirit.

Only when the moon appears, its fullness shaved by two nights, does the will to move arrive. She loads the coffee maker into her trunk. The neighborhood, home to many young families, is accusingly silent, her engine rude. GPS guides her to Jamaica Plain not far from the Arnold Arboretum. She circles for a parking place and finally finds one along the edge of the fenced Arboretum, a short walk from Dan's. His neighborhood, too, is drowsy on a Sunday night. She humps the box through the silent streets like a criminal transporting stolen goods under cover of darkness. But no criminal in her right mind would choose to operate under such a bright moon.

She stands on the sidewalk in front of his building and stares up at the lights on the second floor of his duplex. She has never been here before. She half expects him to appear at the window and spot her. He doesn't, so she rings. A staircase leads up to his second-floor apartment. At the top, a closed door. The door opens and he looks down. When he sees her waving, he descends.

"Hey there, stranger," he says, more surprised than he was at the party.

"I brought you something." She points to the box on the stoop. "A coffee maker I got for my mother, but her boyfriend already got her the same one, a better model."

"Jeez. I'm flattered. Your mother's cast-off."

"Since you're birthday twins you have the right of first refusal."

A moment of silence passes. He looks down at the box. She looks at him.

Her Boys

"I probably shouldn't take it. I'm going to be moving in a couple of months. I'm kind of trying to offload stuff."

You can't just pretend? He has left the door at the top of the stairs open and light jazz wends down, along with voices.

"Nonstop celebrating?" she says.

"Come on up."

"I'm going to get going." She bends for the box.

"Look, I know you're pissed. I should have told you before. I shouldn't have surprised you like that. My bad."

"It's always temporary, Dan. I told you that when I hired you."

He nods. "But it was good. I liked it. It's a great magazine and the stuff we did together, you know, it was all good."

Not good enough, apparently. Hiking the box to her chest, she turns to go, catching Adrian in her peripheral vision peering through the doorway at the top of the stairs. "What's up, mate?" he calls down.

She doesn't wait to find out if he sees her, doesn't wait to find out who else is up there who isn't she. She speed-walks to the corner, box crushed to her chest. Huffing, she stops. She sets the box down. $89 worth of coffeemaker and still not the best. She crosses the street, disowning the box without a glance back. Someone will score. Someone is always scoring. A certain kind of person with a strong independent will who, instead of waiting for things to unfold, pounces. Even her erstwhile-loser brother has become a pouncer.

She follows the iron fence of the arboretum, under the spill of moonlight. She's glad she's not bald. Tiny white petals from some early flowering tree litter the sidewalk. They're probably beautiful if examined closely, no doubt delicate and perfectly shaped, but from her height they're ordinary looking, even messy. Tiny as they are, they're ephemeral, and she steps on them without remorse, the waning moonlight raining down without mercy. She imagines she's already wearing the red leather jacket and absorbing the warm pulse of the creature whose skin it once was.

Publication History

"The Deed" was published in *Arts and Letters: A Journal of Contemporary Culture*

"Vanishing" was published in *TriQuarterly*

"Redhead" was published in *The Santa Monica Review*

"Fat" was a finalist in the *Missouri Review's* Jeffrey Smith's Editor's Prize Contest

"Her Boys" was a finalist in *Narrative Magazine's* Story Contest

The Author

Cai Emmons, winner of the 2018 Leapfrog Fiction Contest for *Vanishing*, is the author of the novels *His Mother's Son, The Stylist*, and *Weather Woman*. A sequel to *Weather Woman, Sinking Islands*, is forthcoming in 2021. Before turning to fiction, Emmons was a dramatist. She has taught at various colleges and universities, most recently at the University of Oregon's Creative Writing Program. She is now a full-time writer.